NORA ROBERTS

LANGUAGE OF LOVE

HER MOTHER'S KEEPER

Silhouette® Books

Published by Silhouette Books New York

America's Publisher of Contemporary Romance

If you purchased this book without a cover you should be aware
that this book is stolen property. It was reported as "unsold and
destroyed" to the publisher, and neither the author nor the
publisher has received any payment for this "stripped book."

SILHOUETTE BOOKS
300 East 42nd St., New York, N.Y. 10017

HER MOTHER'S KEEPER © 1983 by Nora Roberts.
First published as a Silhouette Romance.

Language of Love edition published November 1992

ISBN: 0-373-51020-9

All rights reserved. Except for use in any review,
the reproduction or utilization of this work in
whole or in part in any form by any electronic,
mechanical or other means, now known or
hereafter invented, including xerography,
photocopying and recording, or in any information
storage or retrieval system, is forbidden without
the permission of the publisher, Silhouette Books,
300 E. 42nd Street, New York, N.Y. 10017

All the characters in this book have no existence
outside the imagination of the author and have
no relation whatsoever to anyone bearing the same
name or names. They are not even distantly
inspired by any individual known or unknown
to the author, and all incidents are pure invention.

® are Trademarks registered in the United States Patent
and Trademark Office, the Canada Trade Mark Office
and in other countries.

Printed in U.S.A.

Chapter One

The taxi zipped through the airport traffic. Gwen let out a long sigh as the Louisiana heat throbbed around her. She shifted as the thin material of her ivory lawn blouse dampened against her back. The relief was brief. Squinting out of the window, she decided the July sun hadn't changed in the two years she had been away. The cab veered away from downtown New Orleans and cruised south. Gwen reflected that very little else here had changed in the past two years but herself. Spanish moss still draped the roadside trees, giving even the sun-drenched afternoon a dreamlike effect. The warm, thick scent of flowers still wafted through the air. The atmosphere was touched with an easygoing indolence she nearly had forgotten during the two years she'd spent in Manhattan. Yes, she mused, craning her neck to catch a glimpse of a sheltered bayou, I'm the one who's changed. I've grown up.

When she had left Louisiana, she'd been twenty-one and a starry-eyed innocent. Now, at twenty-three, she felt mature and experienced. As an assistant to the fashion editor of *Style* magazine, Gwen had learned how to cope with deadlines, soothe ruffled models, and squeeze in a personal life around her professional one. More, she had learned how to cope alone, without the comfort of familiar people and places. The gnawing ache of homesickness she had experienced during her first months in New York was forgotten, the torture of insecurity and outright fear of being alone were banished from her memory. Gwen Lacrosse had not merely survived the transplant from magnolias to concrete, she felt she had triumphed. This is one small-town southern girl who can take care of herself, she reflected with a flash of defiance. Gwen had come home not merely for a visit, a summer sabbatical. She had come on a mission. She folded her arms across her chest in an unconscious gesture of determination.

In the rear-view mirror, the taxi driver caught a glimpse of a long, oval face surrounded by a shoulder-length mass of caramel curls. The bone structure of his passenger's face was elegant, but the rather sharp features were set in grim lines. Her huge brown eyes were focused on some middle distance, and her full, wide mouth was unsmiling. In spite of her severe expression, the cabbie decided, the face was a winner. Unaware of the scrutiny, Gwen continued to frown, absorbed by her thoughts. The landscape blurred, then disappeared from her vision.

How, she wondered, could a forty-seven-year-old woman be so utterly naive? What a fool she must be making of herself. Mama's always been dreamy and impractical, but this! It's all *his* fault, she thought resentfully. Her eyes narrowed as she felt a fresh surge of temper, and color rose to warm the ivory tone of her skin. *Luke Powers*—Gwen gritted her teeth on the name—successful novelist and screenwriter, sought-after bachelor and globe-trotter. *And rat,* Gwen added, unconsciously twisting her leather clutch bag in a movement suspiciously akin to that of wringing a neck. A thirty-five-year-old rat. Well, Mr. Powers, Gwen's thoughts continued, your little romance with my mother is through. I've come all these miles to send you packing. And by hook or crook, fair means or foul, that's what I'm going to do.

Gwen sat back, blew the fringe of curls from her eyes and contemplated the pleasure of ousting Luke Powers from her mother's life. Researching a new book, she sniffed. He'll have to research his book without researching my mother. She frowned, remembering the correspondence from her mother over the past three months. Luke Powers had been mentioned on almost every page of the violet-scented paper; helping her mother garden, taking her to the theater, hammering nails, making himself generally indispensable.

At first Gwen had paid little attention to the constant references to Luke. She was accustomed to her mother's enthusiasm for people, her flowery, sentimental outlook. And, to be honest, Gwen reflected with a sigh, I've been preoccupied with my own life, my own problems. Her thoughts flitted back to Michael Palmer—practical, brilliant, selfish, dependable Michael. A small cloud of depression threatened to descend on her as she remembered how miserably she had failed in their relationship. He deserved more than I could give him, she reflected sadly. Her eyes became troubled as she thought of her inability to share herself as Michael had wanted. Body and mind, she had held back both, unwilling or unable to make the commitment. Quickly shaking off the encroaching mood, Gwen reminded herself that while she had failed with Michael, she was succeeding in her career.

In the eyes of most people, the fashion world was glamorous, elegant, full of beautiful people moving gaily from one party to the next. Gwen almost laughed out loud at the absurdity of the illusion. What it really was, as she had since learned, was crazy, frantic, grueling work filled with temperamental artists, high-strung models and impossible deadlines. And I'm good at handling all of them, she mused, automatically straightening her shoulders. Gwen Lacrosse was not afraid of hard work any more than she was afraid of a challenge.

Her thoughts made a quick U-turn back to Luke Powers. There was too much affection in her mother's words when she wrote of him, and his name cropped up too often for comfort. Over the past three months, Gwen's concern had deepened to worry, until she felt she had to do something about the situation and had arranged for a leave of absence. It was, she had decided, up to her to protect her mother from a womanizer like Luke Powers.

She was not intimidated by his reputation with words or his reputation with women. He might be said to be an expert with both, she mused, but I know how to take care of myself and my mother. Mama's trouble is that she's too trusting. She sees only what she wants to see. She doesn't like to see faults. Gwen's mouth softened into a smile, and her face was suddenly, unexpectedly breathtaking. I'll take care of her, she thought confidently, I always have.

The lane leading to Gwen's childhood home was lined with fragile magnolia trees. As the taxi turned in and drove through patches of fragrant shade, Gwen felt the first stirrings of genuine pleasure. The scent of wisteria reached her before her first glimpse of the house. It had three graceful stories and was made of white-washed brick with high French windows and iron balconies like lacework. A veranda flowed across the entire front of the house, where the wisteria was free to climb on trellises at each end. It was not as old or as elaborate as many other antebellum houses in Louisiana, but it had the charm and grace so typical of that period. Gwen felt that the house suited her mother to perfection. They were both fragile, impractical and appealing.

She glanced up at the third story as the taxi neared the end of the drive. The top floor contained four small suites that had been remodeled for "visitors" as her mother called them, or as Gwen more accurately termed them, boarders. The visitors, with their monetary contributions, made it possible to keep the house in the family and in repair. Gwen had grown up with these visitors, accepting them as one accepts a small itch. Now, however, she scowled up at the third-floor windows. One of the suites housed Luke Powers. Not for long, she vowed, as she slipped out of the cab with her chin thrust forward.

As she paid her fare, Gwen glanced absently toward the sound of a low, monotonous thudding. In the side yard, just past a flourishing camellia, a man was in the process of chopping down a long-dead oak. He was stripped to the waist, and his jeans were snug over narrow hips and worn low enough to show a hint of tan line. His back and arms were bronzed and muscled and gleaming with sweat. His hair was a rich brown, touched with lighter streaks that showed a preference for sun. It curled damply at his neck and over his brow.

There was something confident and efficient in his stance. His legs were planted firmly, his swing effortless. Though she could not see his face, she knew he was enjoying his task: the heat, the sweat, the challenge. She stood in the drive as the cab drove off and admired his raw, basic masculinity, the arrogant efficiency of his movements. The axe swung into the heart of the tree with a violent grace. It occurred to her suddenly that for months she had not seen a man do anything more physical than jog in Central Park. Her lips curved in approval and admiration as she watched the rise and fall of the axe, the tensing and flow of muscle. The axe, tree and man were a perfect whole, elemental and beautiful. Gwen had forgotten how beautiful simplicity could be.

The tree shuddered and moaned, then hesitated briefly before it swayed and toppled to the ground. There was a quick whoosh and thump. Gwen felt a ridiculous urge to applaud.

"You didn't say timber," she called out.

He had lifted a forearm to wipe the sweat from his brow and at her call, turned. The sun streamed behind his back. Squinting against it, Gwen could not see his face clearly. There was an aura of light around him, etching the tall, lean body and thickly curling hair. He looks like a god, she thought, like some primitive god of virility. As she watched, he leaned the axe against the stump of the tree and walked toward her. He moved like a man more used to walking on sand or grass than on concrete. Ridiculously, Gwen felt as though she were being stalked. She attributed the strange thrill she felt to the fact that she could not yet make out his features. He was a faceless man, therefore somehow the embodiment of man, exciting and strong. In defense against the glare of the sun, she shaded her eyes with her hand.

"You did that very well." Gwen smiled, attracted by his uncomplicated masculinity. She had not realized how bored she had become with three-piece suits and smooth hands. "I hope you don't mind an audience."

"No. Not everyone appreciates a well-cut tree." His voice was not indolent with vowels. There was nothing of Louisiana in his tone. As his face at last came into focus, Gwen was struck with its power. It was narrow and chiseled, long boned and with the faintest of clefts in the chin. He had not shaved, but the shadow of beard intensified the masculinity of the face. His eyes were a clear blue-gray. They were calm, almost startlingly intelligent under rough brows. It was a calm that suggested power, a calm that captivated the onlooker. Immediately, Gwen knew he was a man who understood himself. Though intrigued, she felt discomfort under the directness of his gaze. She was almost sure he could see beyond her words and into her thoughts.

"I'd say you have definite talent," she told him. There was an aloofness about him, she decided, but it was not the cold aloofness of disinterest. He has warmth, she thought, but he's careful about who receives it. "I'm sure I've never seen a tree toppled with such finesse." She gave him a generous smile. "It's a hot day for axe swinging."

"You've got too many clothes on," he returned simply. His eyes swept down her blouse and skirt and trim, stockinged legs, then up again to her face. It was neither an insolent assessment nor an admiring one; it was simply a statement. Gwen kept her eyes level with his and prayed she would not do anything as foolish as blushing.

"More suitable for plane travelling than tree chopping I suppose," she replied. The annoyance in her voice brought a smile to the corners of his mouth. Gwen reached for her bags, but her hand met his on the handle. She jerked away and stepped back as a new source of heat shot through her. It seemed to dart up her fingers, then explode. Stunned by her own reaction, she stared into his calm eyes. Confusion flitted across her face and creased her brow before she smoothed it away. Silly, she told herself as she struggled to steady her pulse. Absolutely silly. He watched the shock, confusion and annoyance move across her face. Like a mirror, her eyes reflected each emotion.

"Thank you," Gwen said, regaining her poise. "I don't want to take you away from your work."

"No hurry." He hoisted her heavy bags easily. As he moved up the flagstone walk, she fell into step beside him. Even in heels, she barely reached his shoulder. Gwen glanced up to see the sun play on the blond highlights in his hair.

"Have you been here long?" she asked as they mounted the steps to the veranda.

"Few months." He set down her bags and placed his hand on the knob. Pausing, he studied her face with exacting care. Gwen felt her lips curve for no reason at all. "You're much lovelier than your picture, Gwenivere," he said unexpectedly. "Much warmer, much more vulnerable." With a quick twist, he opened the door, then again picked up her bags.

Breaking out of her trance, Gwen followed him inside, reaching for his arm. "How do you know my name?" she demanded. His words left her puzzled and defenseless. He saw too much too quickly.

"Your mother talks of you constantly," he explained as he set her bags down in the cool, white-walled hallway. "She's very proud of you." When he lifted her chin with his fingers, Gwen was too surprised to protest.

"Your beauty is very different from hers. Hers is softer, less demanding, more comfortable. I doubt very much that you inspire comfort in a man." His eyes were on her face again, and fascinated, Gwen stood still. She could nearly feel the heat flowing from his body into hers. "She worries about you being alone in New York."

"One can't be alone in New York, it's a contradiction in terms." A frown shadowed her eyes and touched her mouth with a pout. "She's never told me she worried."

"Of course not, then you'd worry about her worrying." He grinned.

Resolutely Gwen ignored the tingle of pleasure his touch gave her. "You seem to know my mother quite well." Her frown deepened and spread. The grin reminded her of someone. It was charming and almost irresistible. Recognition struck like a thunderbolt. *"You're Luke Powers,"* she accused.

"Yes." His brows lifted at the tone of her voice, and his head tilted slightly as if to gain a new perspective. "Didn't you like my last book?"

"It's your current one I object to," Gwen snapped. She jerked her chin from his hold.

"Oh?" There was both amusement and curiosity in the word.

"To the fact that you're writing it here, in this house," Gwen elaborated.

"Have you a moral objection to my book, Gwenivere?"

"I doubt you know anything about morals," Gwen tossed back as her eyes grew stormy. "And don't call me that, no one but my mother calls me that."

"Pity, such a romantic name," he said casually. "Or do you object to romance as well?"

"When it's between my mother and a Hollywood Casanova a dozen years younger than she, I have a different name for it." Gwen's face flushed with the passion of her words. She stood rigid. The humor faded from Luke's face. Slowly, he tucked his hands in his pockets.

"I see. Would you care to tell me what you'd call it?"

"I won't glorify your conduct with a title," Gwen retorted. "It should be sufficient that you understand I won't tolerate it any longer." She turned, intending to walk away from him.

"Won't you?" There was something dangerously cold in his tone. "And your mother has no voice in the matter?"

"My mother," Gwen countered furiously, "is too gentle, too trusting and too naive." Whirling, she faced him again. "I won't let you make a fool of her."

"My dear Gwenivere," he said smoothly. "You do so well making one of yourself."

Before Gwen could retort, there was the sharp click of heels on wood. Struggling to steady her breathing, Gwen moved down the hall to greet her mother.

"Mama." She embraced a soft bundle of curves smelling of lilac.

"Gwenivere!" Her mother's voice was low and as sweet as the scent she habitually wore. "Why, darling, what are you doing here?"

"Mama," Gwen repeated and pulled away far enough to study the rosy loveliness of her mother's face. Her mother's skin was creamy and almost perfectly smooth, her eyes round and china blue, her nose tilted, her mouth pink and soft. There were two tiny dimples in her cheeks. Looking at her sweet prettiness, Gwen felt their roles should have been reversed. "Didn't you get my letter?" She tucked a stray wisp of pale blond hair behind her mother's ear.

"Of course, you said you'd be here Friday."

Gwen smiled and kissed a dimpled cheek. "This is Friday, Mama."

"Well, yes, it's *this* Friday, but I assumed you meant *next* Friday, and . . . Oh dear, what does it matter?" Anabelle brushed away confusion with the back of her hand. "Let me look at you," she requested and, stepping back, subjected Gwen to a critical study. She saw a tall, striking beauty who brought misty memories of her young husband. Widowed for more than two decades, Anabelle rarely thought of her late husband unless reminded by her daughter. "So thin," she clucked and sighed. "Don't you eat up there?"

"Now and again." Pausing, Gwen made her own survey of her mother's soft, round curves. How could this woman be approaching fifty? she wondered with a surge of pride and awe. "You look wonderful," Gwen murmured, "but then, you always look wonderful."

Anabelle laughed her young, gay laugh. "It's the climate," she claimed as she patted

Gwen's cheek. "None of that dreadful smog or awful snow you have up there." New York, Gwen noted, would always be "up there."

"Oh, Luke!" Anabelle caught sight of him as he stood watching the reunion. A smile lit up her face. "Have you met my Gwenivere?"

Luke shifted his gaze until his eyes met Gwen's. His brow tilted slightly in acknowledgement. "Yes." Gwen thought his smile was as much a challenge as a glove slapped across her cheek. "Gwen and I are practically old friends."

"That's right." Gwen let her smile answer his. "Already we know each other quite well."

"Marvelous." Anabelle beamed. "I do want you two to get along." She gave Gwen's hand a happy squeeze. "Would you like to freshen up, darling, or would you like a cup of coffee first?"

Gwen struggled to keep her voice from trembling with rage as Luke continued to smile at her. "Coffee sounds perfect," she answered.

"I'll take your bags up," Luke offered as he lifted them again.

"Thank you, dear." Anabelle spoke before Gwen could refuse. "Try to avoid Miss Wilkins until you have a shirt on. The sight of all those muscles will certainly give her the vapors. Miss Wilkins is one of my visitors," Anabelle explained as she led Gwen down the hall. "A sweet, timid little soul who paints in watercolors."

"Hmm," Gwen answered noncommittally as she glanced back over her shoulder. Luke stood watching them with sunlight tumbling over his hair and bronzed skin. "Hmm," Gwen said again and turned away.

The kitchen was exactly as Gwen remembered; big, sunny and spotlessly clean. Tillie, the tall, waspishly thin cook stood by the stove. "Hello, Miss Gwen," she said without turning around. "Coffee's on."

"Hello, Tillie." Gwen walked over to the stove and sniffed at the fragrant steam. "Smells good."

"Cajun jambalaya."

"My favorite," Gwen murmured, glancing up at the appealingly ugly face. "I thought I wasn't expected until next Friday."

"You weren't," Tillie agreed, with a sniff. Lowering her thick brows, she continued to stir the roux.

Gwen smiled and leaned over to peck Tillie's tough cheek. "How are things, Tillie?"

"Comme ci, comme ça," she muttered, but pleasure touched her cheeks with color. Turning, she gave Gwen a quick study. "Skinny," was her quick, uncomplimentary conclusion.

"So I'm told." Gwen shrugged. Tillie never flattered anyone. "You have a month to fatten me up."

"Isn't that marvellous, Tillie?" Anabelle carefully put a blue delft sugar and creamer set on the kitchen table. "Gwen is staying for an entire month. Perhaps we should have a party! We have three visitors at the moment. Luke, of course, and Miss Wilkins and Mr. Stapleton. He's an artist, too, but he works in oils. Quite a talented young man."

Gwen seized the small opening. "Luke Powers is considered a gifted young man, too." She sat across from her mother as Anabelle poured the coffee.

"Luke *is* frightfully talented," Anabelle agreed with a proud sigh. "Surely you've read some of his books, seen some of his movies? Overwhelming. His characters are so real, so vital. His romantic scenes have a beauty and intensity that just leave me weak."

"He had a naked woman in one of his movies," Tillie stated in an indignant mutter. "Stark naked."

Anabelle laughed. Her eyes smiled at Gwen's over the rim of her cup. "Tillie feels Luke is singlehandedly responsible for the moral decline in the theater," Belle continued.

"Not a stitch on," Tillie added, setting her chin.

Though Gwen was certain Luke Powers had no morals whatsoever, she made no reference to them. Her voice remained casual as instead she commented, "He certainly has accomplished quite a bit for a man of his age. A string of best-sellers, a clutch of popular movies . . . and he's only thirty-five."

"I suppose that shows how unimportant age really is," Anabelle said serenely. Gwen barely suppressed a wince. "And success hasn't spoiled him one little bit," she went on. "He's the kindest, sweetest man I've ever known. He's so generous with his time, with himself." Her eyes shone with emotion. "I can't tell you how good he's been for me. I feel like a new woman." Gwen choked on her coffee. Anabelle clucked in sympathy as Tillie gave Gwen a sturdy thump on the back. "Are you all right, honey?"

"Yes, yes, I'm fine." Gwen took three deep breaths to steady her voice. Looking into her mother's guileless blue eyes, she opted for a temporary retreat. "I think I'll go upstairs and unpack."

"I'll help you," Anabelle volunteered and started to rise.

"No, no, don't bother." Gwen placed a gentle hand on her shoulder. "It won't take long. I'll shower and change and be down in an hour." In an hour, Gwen hoped to have her thoughts more in order. She looked down at her mother's smooth, lovely face and felt a hundred years old. "I love you, Mama," she sighed, and kissed Anabelle's brow before she left her.

As Gwen moved down the hall, she realigned her strategy. Obviously, there was little she could say to her mother that would discourage her relationship with Luke Powers. It was going to be necessary, she decided, to go straight to the source. While climbing the stairs, she searched her imagination for an appropriate name for him. She could find nothing vile enough.

Chapter Two

A shaft of sunlight poured over the floor in Gwen's room. The walls were covered in delicate floral paper. Eggshell-tinted sheer curtains were draped at the windows, matching the coverlet on the four-poster bed. As she always did when she entered the room, Gwen crossed to the French windows and threw them open. Scents from Anabelle's flower garden swam up to meet her. Across the lawn was a spreading cypress, older than the house it guarded, festooned with gray green moss. The sun filtered through it, making spiderweb patterns on the ground. Bird song melded with the drone of bees. She could barely glimpse the mystery of the bayou through a thick curtain of oaks. New York's busy streets seemed nonexistent. Gwen had chosen that world for its challenges, but she discovered that coming home was like a sweet dessert after a full meal. She had missed its taste. Feeling unaccountably more lighthearted, she turned back into her room. She plucked up her white terry-cloth robe and headed for the shower.

Mama's romanticizing again, Gwen mused as the water washed away her travel weariness. She simply doesn't understand men at all. *And you do?* her conscience asked as she thought uncomfortably of Michael. Yes, I do understand them, she answered defiantly as she held her face up to the spray. I understand them perfectly. I won't let Luke hurt my mother, she vowed. I won't let him make a fool of her. I suppose he's used to getting his own way because he's successful and attractive. Well, I deal with successful, attractive people every day, and I know precisely how to handle them. Refreshed and ready for battle, Gwen stepped from the shower. With her confidence restored, she hummed lightly as she towel-dried her hair. Curls sprang to life on her forehead. Slipping on her robe, she tied the belt at her waist and strolled back into the bedroom.

"You!" Gwen jerked the knot tight as she spied Luke Powers standing beside her dresser. "What are you doing in my room?"

Calmly, his eyes traveled over her. The frayed robe was short, revealing slender legs well above the knee. Its simplicity outlined her nearly boyish slenderness. Without makeup, her eyes were huge and dark and curiously sweet. Luke watched her damp curls bounce with the outraged toss of her head.

"Anabelle thought you'd like these," he said as he indicated a vase of fresh yellow roses on the dresser. His hand made the gesture, but his eyes remained on Gwen. Gwen frowned.

"You should have knocked," she said ungraciously.

"I did," he said easily. "You didn't answer." To her amazement, he crossed the distance between them and lifted a hand to her cheek. "You have incredibly beautiful skin. Like rose petals washed in rainwater."

"Don't!" Knocking his hand away, Gwen stepped back. "Don't touch me." She pushed her hair away from her face.

Luke's eyes narrowed fractionally at her tone, but his voice was calm. "I always touch what I admire."

"I don't want you to admire me."

Humor lit his face and added to its appeal. "I didn't say I admired you, Gwen, I said I admired your skin."

"Just keep your hands off my skin," she snapped, wishing the warmth of his fingers would evaporate and leave her cheek as it had been before his touch. "And keep your hands off my mother."

"What gives you the notion I've had my hands on your mother?" Luke inquired, lifting a bottle of Gwen's scent and examining it.

"Her letters were clear enough." Gwen snatched the bottle from him and slammed it back on the dresser. "They've been full of nothing but you for months. How you went to the theater or shopping, how you fixed her car or sprayed the peach trees. Especially how you've given her life fresh meaning." Agitated, Gwen picked up her comb, then put it down again. His direct, unruffled stare tripped her nerves.

"And from that," Luke said into the silence, "you've concluded that Anabelle and I are having an affair."

"Well, of course." His tone confused her for a moment. Was he amused? she wondered. His mouth was beautiful, a smile lurking on it. Furious with herself, Gwen tilted her chin. "Do you deny it?"

Luke slipped his hands into his pockets and wandered about the room. Pausing, he studied the view from the open French windows. "No, I don't believe I will. I believe I'll simply tell you it's none of your business."

"None of my..." Gwen sputtered, then swallowed in a torrent of fury. "None of my business? She's my mother!"

"She's also a person," Luke cut in. When he turned back to face her, there was curiosity on his face. "Or don't you ever see her that way?"

"I don't feel it's—"

"No, you probably don't," he interrupted. "It's certainly time you did though. I doubt you feel Anabelle should approve of every man you have a relationship with."

Color flared in Gwen's cheeks. "That's entirely different," she fumed, then stalked over to stand in front of him. "I don't need you to tell me about my mother. You can flaunt your affairs with actresses and socialites all you want, but—"

"Thank you," Luke replied evenly. "It's nice to have your approval."

"I won't have you flaunting your affair with my mother," Gwen finished between her teeth. "You should be ashamed," she added with a toss of her head, "seducing a woman a dozen years older than you."

"Of course, it would be perfectly acceptable if I were a dozen years older than she," he countered smoothly.

"I didn't *say* that," Gwen began. Her brow creased with annoyance.

"You look too intelligent to hold such views, Gwen. You surprise me." His mild voice was infuriating.

"I don't!" she denied hotly. Because the thought made her uncomfortable, her mouth moved into a pout. Luke's eyes dropped to her lips and lingered.

"A very provocative expression," he said softly. "I thought so the first time I saw it, and it continues to intrigue me." In one swift motion, he gathered her into his arms. At her gasp of surprised protest, he merely smiled. "I told you I always touch what I admire." Gwen squirmed, but she was pinned tight against him, helpless as his face lowered toward her.

His lips feathered lightly along her jawline. Gwen was caught off guard by the gentleness. Though his chest was solid and strong against her yielding breasts, his mouth was soft and sweet. Disarmed, she stood still in the circle of his arms as his mouth roamed her face. Through the slight barrier of the robe, she could feel every line of his body. They merged together as if destined to do so. Heat began to rise in her, a sudden, unexpected heat as irresistible as his mouth. Her lips throbbed for the touch of his. She moaned softly as he continued to trace light, teasing kisses over her skin. Her hands slipped up from his chest to find their way into his hair, urging him to fulfill a silent promise. At last his lips brushed hers. They touched, then clung, then devoured.

Lost in pleasure, riding on sensations delirious and new, Gwen answered his demands with fervor. She rose on her toes to meet them. The kiss grew deeper. The roughness of his beard scratched her skin and tripled her heartbeat. A tenuous breeze fanned the curtains at the open windows, but Gwen felt no lessening of heat. Luke moved his hands down her spine, firmly caressing her curves before he took her hips and drew her away.

Gwen stared up at him with dark, cloudy eyes. Never had a kiss moved her more, never had she been so filled with fire and need. Her soft mouth trembled with desire for his. The knowledge of what could be hers lay just beyond her comprehension. Luke lifted his hand to her damp curls, tilting back her head for one last, brief kiss. "You taste every bit as good as you look."

Abruptly Gwen remembered who and where she was. The fires of passion were extinguished by fury. "Oh!" She gave Luke's chest a fierce push and succeeded in putting an entire inch between them. "How could you?"

"It wasn't hard," he assured her.

Gwen shook her head. Tiny droplets of water danced in the sunlight. "You're despicable!"

"Why?" Luke's smile broadened. "Because I made you forget yourself for a moment? You made me forget myself for a moment too." He seemed to enjoy the confession. "Does that make you despicable?"

"I didn't ... It was you ... I just ..." Her words stumbled to a halt, and she made ineffectual noises in her throat.

"At least try to be coherent," Luke said.

"Just let me go," Gwen demanded. She began a violent and fruitless struggle. "Just let me go!"

"Certainly," Luke obliged. He brushed back her disheveled hair with a friendly hand. "You know, one day you might just be the woman your mother is."

"Oh!" Gwen paled in fury. "You're disgusting."

Luke laughed with pure masculine enjoyment. "Gwenivere, I wasn't speaking of your rather exceptional physical virtues." He sobered, then shook his head. "Anabelle is the only person I know who looks for the good in everyone and finds it. It's her most attractive asset." His eyes were calm again and thoughtful. "Perhaps you should take time to get to know your mother while you're here. You might be surprised."

Gwen retreated behind a film of ice. "I told you, I don't need you to tell me about my mother."

"No?" Luke smiled, shrugged, and moved to the door. "Perhaps I'll spend my time teaching you about yourself then. See you at dinner." He closed the door on her furious retort.

The front parlor had both the color and the scent of roses. It was furnished in Anabelle's delicate and feminine style. The chairs were small and elegant with dusky pink cushions; the lamps, china and terrifyingly fragile; the rugs, faded and French. Even when she was not there, Anabelle's presence could be felt.

Gwen pushed aside a pale pink curtain and watched the sun go down while Anabelle chattered happily. The sky gradually took on the hues of sunset, until it glowed with defiant gold and fiery reds. Its passion suited Gwen much more than the soft comfort of the room at her back. She lifted her palm to the glass of the window as if to touch that explosion of nature. She still felt the aftershocks of the explosion that had burst inside her only a few hours before in the arms of a stranger.

It meant nothing, she assured herself for the hundredth time. I was off guard, tired, confused. I'm sure most of what I felt was pure imagination. I'm on edge, that's all, everything's exaggerated. She ran the tip of her tongue experimentally along her lips, but found no remnants of the heady flavor she remembered. Exaggerated, she told herself again.

"A month's quite a long time for you to be away from your job," Anabelle said conversationally as she sorted through a basket of embroidery thread.

Gwen shrugged and made a small sound of agreement. "I haven't taken more than a long weekend in nearly two years."

"Yes, darling, I know. You work too hard."

The cerulean blue dress suited Gwen well, but as Anabelle glanced up at her, she again thought how thin her daughter looked. She was slim and straight as a wand. Gwen's hair caught some of the last flames of the sun, and the mass of curls became a flood of rose-gold light. *How did she get to be twenty-three?* Anabelle wondered. She went back to sorting her thread. "You always were an overachiever. You must get that from your father's side. His mother had two sets of twins, you know. That's overachievement."

With a laugh, Gwen rested her forehead against the glass of the window. It was as refreshing as her mother. "Oh, Mama, I do love you."

"I love you too, dear," she answered absently as she scrutinized two tones of green. "You haven't mentioned that young man you were seeing, the attorney. Michael, wasn't it?"

"It was," Gwen returned dryly. Dusk began to fall as she watched. With the mellowing of light came an odd, almost reverent hush. She sighed. Dusk, she thought, was the most precious time and the most fleeting. The sound of the first cricket brought her out of her reverie. "I'm not seeing Michael anymore."

"Oh dear." Anabelle looked up, distressed. "Did you have a disagreement?"

"A series of them. I'm afraid I don't make the ideal companion for a corporate attorney." Gwen made a face in the glass and watched it reflect. "I have too many deep-rooted plebeian values. Mostly, I like to see the little guy get a break."

"Well, I hope you parted friends."

Gwen closed her eyes and stifled a sardonic laugh as she recalled the volatile parting scene. "I'm sure we'll exchange Christmas cards for years to come."

"That's nice," Anabelle murmured comfortably as she threaded her needle. "Old friends are the most precious."

With a brilliant smile, Gwen turned toward her mother. The smile faded instantly as she spotted Luke in the doorway. As her eyes locked with his, she felt herself trembling. He had changed into tan slacks and a rust-colored shirt. The effect was casual and expensive. But somehow there seemed little difference between the clean-shaven, conventionally clad man Gwen now saw and the rugged woodsman she had met that morning. Clothes and a razor could not alter the essence of his virility.

"It's a fortunate man who has two exquisite women to himself."

"Luke!" Anabelle's head lifted. Instantly, her face was touched with pleasure. "How lovely it is to be flattered! Don't you agree, Gwen?"

"Lovely," Gwen assented, as she sent him her most frigid smile.

With easy assurance, Luke crossed the room. From Gwen's grandmother's Hepplewhite server, he lifted a crystal decanter. "Sherry?"

"Thank you, darling." Anabelle turned her smile from him to Gwen. "Luke bought the most delightful sherry. I'm afraid he's been spoiling me."

I'll just bet he has, Gwen muttered silently. Temper flared in her eyes. Had she seen it, Anabelle would have recognized the look. Luke both saw it and recognized it. To Gwen's further fury, he grinned.

"We shouldn't dawdle long," Anabelle said, unconscious of the war being waged over her head. "Tillie has a special supper planned for Gwen. She dotes on her, you know, though she wouldn't admit it for the world. I believe she's missed Gwen every bit as much as I have these past two years."

"She's missed having someone to scold," Gwen smiled ruefully. "I still carry the stigma of being skinny and unladylike that I acquired when I was ten."

"You'll always be ten to Tillie, darling." Anabelle sighed and shook her head. "I have a difficult time realizing you're more than twice that myself.''

Gwen turned toward Luke as he offered her a glass of sherry. "Thank you," she said in her most graciously insulting voice. She sipped, faintly disappointed to find that it was excellent. "And will you be spoiling me as well, Mr. Powers?"

"Oh, I doubt that, Gwenivere." He took her hand, although she stiffened and tried to pull it away. His eyes laughed over their joined fingers. "I doubt that very much."

Chapter Three

Over dinner Gwen met Anabelle's two other visitors. Though both were artists, they could not have been more different from each other. Monica Wilkins was a small, pale woman with indifferent brown hair. She spoke in a quiet, breathy voice and avoided eye contact at all costs. She had a supply of large, shapeless smocks, which she wore invariably and without flair. Her art was, for the most part, confined to illustrating textbooks on botany. With a touch of pity, Gwen noticed that her tiny, birdlike eyes often darted glances at Luke, then shifted away quickly and self-consciously.

Bradley Stapleton was tall and lanky, casually dressed in an ill-fitting sweater, baggy slacks and battered sneakers. He had a cheerful, easily forgettable face and a surprisingly beautiful voice. He studied his fellow humans with unquenchable curiosity and painted for the love of it. He yearned to be famous but had settled for regular meals.

Gwen thoroughly enjoyed dinner, not only because of Tillie's excellent jambalaya but for the oddly interesting company of the two artists. Separately, she thought each might be a bore, but somehow together, the faults of one enhanced the virtues of the other.

"So, you work for *Style,*" Bradley stated as he scooped up a second, generous helping of Tillie's jambalaya. "Why don't you model?"

Gwen thought of the frantic, nervous models with their fabulous faces. She shook her head. "No, I'm not at all suitable. I'm much better at stroking."

"Stroking?" Bradley repeated, intrigued.

"That's what I do basically." Gwen smiled at him. It was better, she decided, that her mother had seated her next to Luke rather than across from him. She would have found it uncomfortable to face him throughout an entire meal. "Soothe, stroke, bully. Someone has to keep the models from using their elegant nails on each other and remind them of the practical side of life."

"Gwen's so good at being practical," Anabelle interjected. "I'm sure I don't understand why. I've never been. Strange," she said, and smiled at her daughter. "She grew up long before I did."

"Practicality wouldn't suit you, Anabelle," Luke told her with an affectionate smile.

Anabelle dimpled with pleasure. "I told you he was spoiling me," she said to Gwen.

"So you did." Gwen lifted her water glass and sipped carefully.

"You must sit for me, Gwen," Bradley said, as he buttered a biscuit.

"Must I?" Knowing the only way she could get through a civilized meal was to ignore Luke, Gwen gave Bradley all her attention.

"Absolutely." Bradley held both the biscuit and knife suspended while he narrowed his eyes and stared at her. "Fabulous, don't you agree, Monica? A marvelous subject," he went on without waiting for her answer. "In some lights the hair would be the color Titian immortalized, in others, it would be quieter, more subtle. But it's the eyes, isn't it, Monica? It's definitely the eyes. So large, so meltingly brown. Of course, the bone structure's perfect, and the skin's wonderful, but I'm taken with the eyes. The lashes are real, too, aren't they, Monica?''

"Yes, quite real," she answered as her gaze flew swiftly to Gwen's face and then back to her plate. "Quite real."

"She gets them from her father," Anabelle explained as she added a sprinkle of salt to her jambalaya. "Such a handsome boy; Gwen favors him remarkably. His eyes were exactly the same. I believe they're why I first fell in love with him."

"They're very alluring," Bradley commented with a nod to Anabelle. "The size, the color, the shape. Very alluring." He faced Gwen again. "You will sit for me, won't you, Gwen?"

Gwen gave Bradley a guileless smile. "Perhaps."

The meal drifted to a close, and the evening waned. The artists retreated to their rooms, and Luke wandered off to his. At Gwen's casual question, Anabelle told her that Luke "worked all the time." It was odd, Gwen mused to herself, that a woman as romantic as her mother wasn't concerned that the man in her life was not spending his evening with her.

Anabelle chattered absently while working tiny, decorative stitches into a pillowcase. Watching her, Gwen was struck with a sudden thought. Did Anabelle seem happier? Did she seem more vital? If Luke Powers was responsible, should she, Gwen, curse him or thank him? She watched Anabelle delicately stifle a yawn and was swept by a fierce, protective surge. She needs me to look out for her, she decided, and that's what I plan to do.

Once in her bedroom, however, Gwen could not get to sleep. The book she had brought with her to pass the time did not hold her attention. It grew late, but her mind would not allow her body to rest. A breeze blew softly in through the windows, lifting the curtains. It beckoned. Rising, Gwen threw on a thin robe and went outside to meet it.

The night was warm and lit by a large summer moon. The air was filled with the scent of wisteria and roses. She could hear the continual hum of the crickets. Now and then, there was the lonely, eerie call of an owl. Leaves rustled with the movements of night birds and small animals. Fireflies blinked and soared.

As Gwen breathed in the moist, fragrant air, an unexpected peace settled over her.

Tranquility was something just remembered, like a childhood friend. Tentatively Gwen reached out for it. For two years, her career had been her highest priority. Independence and success were the goals she had sought. She had worked hard for them. And I've got them, she thought as she plucked a baby coral rose from its bush. Why aren't I happy? I am happy, she corrected as she lifted the bloom and inhaled its fragile scent, but I'm not as happy as I should be. Frowning, she twisted the stem between her fingers. *Complete.* The word came from nowhere. I don't feel complete. With a sigh, she tilted her head and studied the star-studded sky. Laughter bubbled up in her throat suddenly and sounded sweet in the silence.

"Catch!" she cried as she tossed the bloom in the air. She gasped in surprise as a hand plucked the rose on its downward journey. Luke had appeared as if from nowhere and was standing a few feet away from her twirling the flower under his nose. "Thanks," he said softly. "No one has ever tossed me a rose."

"I wasn't tossing it to you." Automatically, Gwen clutched her robe together where it crossed her breasts.

"No?" Luke smiled at her and at the gesture. "Who then?"

Feeling foolish, Gwen shrugged and turned away. "I thought you were working."

"I was. The muse took a break so I called it a night. Gardens are at their best in the moonlight." He paused, and there was an intimacy in his voice. Stepping closer, he added, "I've always thought the same held true for women."

Gwen felt her skin grow warm. She struggled to keep her tone casual as she turned to face him.

Luke tucked the small flower into her curls and lifted her chin. "They are fabulous eyes, you know. Bradley's quite right."

Her skin began to tingle where his fingers touched it. Defensively, she stepped back. "I wish you wouldn't keep doing that." Her voice trembled, and she despised herself for it.

Luke gave her an odd, amused smile. "You're a strange one, Gwenivere. I haven't got you labeled quite yet. I'm intrigued by the innocence."

Gwen stiffened and tossed back her hair. "I don't know what you're talking about."

Luke's smile broadened. The moonlight seemed trapped in his eyes. "Your New York veneer doesn't cover it. It's in the eyes. Bradley doesn't know why they're appealing, and I won't tell him. It's the innocence and the promise." Gwen frowned, but her shoulders relaxed. Luke went on, "There's an unspoiled innocence in that marvelous face, and a warmth that promises passion. It's a tenuous balance."

His words made Gwen uncomfortable. A warmth was spreading through her that she seemed powerless to control. Tranquility had vanished. An excitement, volatile and hot, throbbed through the air. Suddenly she was afraid. "I don't want you to say these things to me," she whispered and took another step in retreat.

"No?" The amusement in his voice told her that a full retreat would be impossible. "Didn't Michael ever use words to seduce you? Perhaps that's why he failed."

"Michael? What do you know about...?" Abruptly she recalled the conversation with her mother before dinner. "You were listening!'' she began, outraged. ''You had no right to listen to a private conversation! No gentleman listens to a private conversation!''

''Nonsense,'' Luke said calmly. ''Everyone does, if he has the chance.''

''Do you enjoy intruding on other people's privacy?''

''People interest me, emotions interest me. I don't apologize for my interests.''

Gwen was torn between fury at his arrogance and admiration for his confidence. ''What *do* you apologize for, Luke Powers?''

''Very little.''

Unable to do otherwise, Gwen smiled. Really, she thought, he's outrageous.

''Now that was worth waiting for,'' Luke murmured, as his eyes roamed her face. ''I wonder if Bradley can do it justice? Be careful,'' he warned, ''you'll have him falling in love with you.''

''Is that how you won Monica?''

''She's terrified of me,'' Luke corrected as he reached up to better secure the rose in her hair.

''Some terrific observer of humanity you are.'' Gwen sniffed, fiddling with the rose herself and managing to dislodge it. As it tumbled to the ground, both she and Luke stooped to retrieve it. Her hair brushed his cheek before she lifted her eyes to his. As if singed, she jolted back, but before she could escape, he took her arm. Slowly, he rose, bringing her with him. Involuntarily, she shivered as he brought her closer until their bodies touched. Just a look from him, just the touch of him, incited her to a passion that she had not known she possessed. His hands slid up her arms and under the full sleeves of her robe to caress her shoulders. She felt her mantle of control slip away as she swayed forward and touched her lips to his.

His mouth was avid so quickly, her breath caught in her throat. Then all was lost in pleasure. Lights fractured and exploded behind her closed lids as her lips sought to give and to take with an instinct as old as time. Beneath her palms she felt the hard, taut muscles of his back. She shuddered with the knowledge of his strength and the sudden realization of her own frailty. But even her weakness had a power she had never tapped, never experienced.

His hands roamed over her, lighting fires, learning secrets, teaching and taking. Gwen

was pliant and willing. He was like a drug
flowing into her system, clouding her brain.
Only the smallest grain of denial struggled for
survival, fighting against the growing need to
surrender. Reason surfaced slowly, almost re-
luctantly. Suddenly, appalled by her own behavior, she began to struggle. But when she
broke away, she felt a quick stab of loneli-
ness.

"No." Gwen lifted her hands to her burn-
ing cheeks. "No," she faltered.

Luke watched in silence as she turned and
fled to the house.

Chapter Four

The morning was hazy and heavy. So were Gwen's thoughts. As dawn broke with a gray, uncertain light, she stood by her window.

How could I? she demanded of herself yet again. Closing her eyes and groaning, Gwen sank down onto the window seat. I kissed him. *I* kissed *him*. Inherent honesty kept her from shifting what she considered blame. I can't say I was caught off guard this time. I knew what was going to happen, and worse yet, I *enjoyed* it. She brought her knees up to her chin. I enjoyed the first time he kissed me too. The silent admission caused her to shut her eyes again. *How could I?* As she wrestled with this question, she rose and paced the room. I came thousands of miles to get Luke Powers out of Mama's life, and I end up kissing him in the garden in the middle of the night. And liking it, she added wretchedly. What kind of a person am I? What kind of a daughter am I? I never thought of Mama once in that garden last night. Well, I'll think of her today, she asserted, and pulled a pair of olive-drab shorts from her drawer. I've got a month to move Luke Powers out, and that's just what I'm going to do.

As she buttoned up a short-sleeved khaki blouse, Gwen nodded confidently at herself in the mirror. No more moonlit gardens. I won't take the chance of having midsummer madness creep over me again. That's what it was, wasn't it? she asked the slender woman in the glass. She ran a nervous hand through her hair. Another answer seemed just beyond her reach. Refusing any attempt to pursue it, Gwen finished dressing and left the room.

Not even Tillie was in the kitchen at such an early hour. There was a certain enjoyment in being up alone in the softly lit room. She made the first pot of coffee in the gray dawn. She sipped at a cupful while watching dark clouds gather. Rain, she thought, not displeased. The sky promised it, the air smelled of it. It gave an excitement to the quiet, yawning morning. There would be thunder and lightning and cooling wind. The thought inexplicably lifted Gwen's spirits. Humming a cheerful tune, she began searching the cupboards. The restless night was forgotten.

"What are you up to?" Tillie demanded, sweeping into the room. Hands on her bony hips, she watched Gwen.

"Good morning, Tillie." Used to the cook's abrasiveness, Gwen answered good naturedly.

"What do you want in my kitchen?" she asked suspiciously. "You made coffee."

"Yes, it's not too bad." Gwen's tone was apologetic, but her eyes danced with mischief.

"I make the coffee," Tillie reminded her. "I always make the coffee."

"I've certainly missed it over the past couple of years. No matter how I try, mine never tastes quite like yours." Gwen poured a fresh cup. "Have some," she offered. "Maybe you can tell me what I do wrong."

Tillie accepted the cup and scowled. "You let it brew too long," she complained. Lifting her hand, she brushed curls back from Gwen's forehead. "Will you never keep your hair out of your eyes? Do you want to wear glasses?"

"No, Tillie," Gwen answered humbly. It was an old gesture and an old question. She recognized the tenderness behind the brisk words and quick fingers. Her lips curved into a smile. "I made Mama's breakfast." Turning, Gwen began to arrange cups and plates on a tray. "I'm going to take it up to her, she always liked it when I surprised her that way."

"You shouldn't bother your *Maman* so early in the morning," Tillie began.

"Oh, it's not so early," Gwen said airily as she lifted the tray. "I didn't leave much of a mess," she added with the carelessness of youth. "I'll clean it up when I come back." She whisked through the door before Tillie could comment.

Gwen moved quickly up the stairs and down the corridor. Balancing the tray in one hand, she twisted the knob on her mother's door with the other. She was totally stunned to find it locked. Automatically, she jiggled the knob in disbelief. Never, as far back as her childhood memories stretched, did Gwen remember the door of Anabelle's room being locked.

"Mama?" There was a question in her voice as she knocked. "Mama, are you up?"

"What?" Anabelle's voice was clear but distracted. "Oh, Gwen, just a minute, darling."

Gwen stood outside the door listening to small, shuffling sounds she could not identify. "Mama," she said again, "are you all right?"

"Yes, yes, dear, one moment." The creaks and shuffles stopped just before the door opened. "Good morning, Gwen." Anabelle smiled. Though she wore a gown and robe and her hair was mussed by sleep, her eyes were awake and alert. "What have you got there?"

Blankly, Gwen looked down at the tray she carried. "Oh, chocolate and *beignets*. I know how you like them. Mama, what were you...?"

"Darling, how sweet!" Anabelle interrupted and drew Gwen into the room. "Did you really make them yourself? What a treat. Come, let's sit on the balcony. I hope you slept well."

Gwen evaded a lie. "I woke early and decided to test my memory with the *beignet* recipe. Mama, I don't remember you ever locking your door."

"No?" Anabelle smiled as she settled herself in a white, wrought-iron chair. "It must be a new habit then. Oh dear, it looks like rain. Well, my roses will be thankful."

The locked door left Gwen feeling slighted. It reminded her forcibly that Anabelle Lacrosse was a person as well as her mother. Perhaps she would do well to remember it, Gwen silently resolved. She set the tray on a round, glass-topped table and bent to kiss Anabelle's cheek. "I've really missed you. I don't think I've told you that yet."

"Gwenivere." Anabelle smiled and patted her daughter's fine-boned hand. "It's so good to have you home. You've always been such a pleasure to me."

"Even when I'd track mud on the carpet or lose frogs in the parlor?" Grinning, Gwen sat and poured the chocolate.

"Darling." Anabelle sighed and shook her head. "Some things are best forgotten. I never understood how I could have raised such a hooligan. But even as I despaired of you ever being a lady, I couldn't help admiring your freedom of spirit. Hot-tempered you might have been," Anabelle added as she tasted her chocolate, "but never malicious and never dishonest. No matter what dreadful thing you did, you never did it out of spite, and you always confessed."

Gwen laughed. Her curls danced as she tossed back her head. "Poor Mama, I must have done so many dreadful things."

"Well, perhaps a bit more than your share," Anabelle suggested kindly. "But now you're all grown up, so difficult for a mother to accept. Your job, Gwen, you do enjoy it?"

Gwen's automatic agreement faltered on her lips. Enjoy, she thought. I wonder if I do. "Strange," she said aloud, "I'm not at all certain." She gave her mother a puzzled smile. "But I need it, not just for the money, I need the responsibility it imposes, I need to be involved."

"Yes, you always did... My, the *beignets* look marvelous."

"They are," Gwen assured her mother as she rested her elbows on the table and her chin on her open palms. "I felt obligated to try one before I offered them to you."

"See, I've always told you you were sensible," Anabelle said with a smile before she tasted one of the oddly shaped doughnuts. "Delicious," she proclaimed. "Tillie doesn't make them any better, though that had best be our secret."

Gwen allowed time to pass with easy conversation until she poured the second cup of chocolate. "Mama," she began cautiously, "how long does Luke Powers plan to stay here?"

The lifting of Anabelle's delicate brows indicated her surprise. "Stay?" she repeated as she dusted powdered sugar from her fingers. "Why I don't know precisely, Gwen. It depends, I should say, on the stage of his book. I know he plans to finish the first draft before he goes back to California."

"I suppose," Gwen said casually as she stirred her chocolate, "he'll have no reason to come back here after that."

"Oh, I imagine he'll be back." Anabelle smiled into her daughter's eyes. "Luke is very fond of this part of the country. I wish I could tell you what his coming here has meant to me." Dreamily, she stared out into the hazy sky. Gwen felt a stab of alarm. "He's given me so much. I'd like you to spend some time with him, dear, and get to know him."

Gwen's teeth dug into the tender inside of her lip. For the moment, she felt completely at a loss. She raged in silence while Anabelle smiled secretly at rain clouds. Despicable man. How can he do this to her? Gwen glanced down into the dregs of her cup and felt a weight descend on her heart. And what is he doing to me? No matter how she tried to ignore it, Gwen could still feel the warmth of his lips on hers. The feeling clung, taunting and enticing. She was teased by a feeling totally foreign to her, a longing she could neither identify nor understand. Briskly, she shook her head to clear her thoughts. Luke Powers was only a problem while he was in Louisiana. The aim was to get him back to the West coast and to discourage him from coming back.

"Gwen?"

"Hmm? Oh yes, Mama." Blinking away the confused images and thoughts of Luke, Gwen met Anabelle's curious look.

"I said blueberry pie would be nice with supper. Luke's very fond of it. I thought perhaps you'd like to pick some berries for Tillie."

Gwen pondered briefly on the attractive prospect of sprinkling arsenic over Luke's

portion, then rejected the idea. "I'd love to,"
she murmured.

The air was thick with moisture when,
armed with a large bucket, Gwen went in
search of blueberries. With a quick glance and
shrug at the cloudy sky, she opted to risk the
chance of rain. She would use her berry picking time to devise a plan to send Luke Powers
westward. Swinging the bucket, she moved
across the trim lawn and into the dim, shel-
tering trees that formed a border between her
home and the bayou. Here was a different
world from her mother's gentle, tidy well-kept
home. This was a primitive world with ageless secrets and endless demands. It had been
Gwen's refuge as a child, her personal island.
Although she remembered each detail perfectly, she stood and drank in its beauty anew.

There was a mist over the sluggish stream.
Dull and brown, cattails peeked through the
surface in search of the hidden sun. Here and
there, cypress stumps rose above the surface.
The stream itself moved in a narrow path,
then curved out of sight. Gwen remembered
how it twisted and snaked and widened. Over
the straight, slender path, trees arched tun-
nel-like, garnished with moss. The water was

silent, but Gwen could hear the birds and an occasional plop of a frog. She knew the serenity was a surface thing. Beneath the calm was a passive and violence and wild, surging life. It called to her as it always had.

With confidence, she moved along the riverbank and searched out the plump wild berries. Silence and the simplicity of her task were soothing. Years slipped away, and she was a teenager again, a girl whose most precious fantasy was to be a part of a big city. She had dreamed in the sheltered bayou of the excitement, the mysteries of city life, the challenges of carving out her own path. Hard work, determination and a quick mind had hurried her along that path. She had earned a responsible job, established an interesting circle of friends and acquired just lately a nagging sense of dissatisfaction.

Overwork, Gwen self-diagnosed, and popped a berry into her mouth. Its juice was sweet and full of memories. And, of course, there's Michael. With a frown, Gwen dropped a handful of berries into the bucket. *Even though it was my idea to end things between us, I could be suffering from the backlash of a terminated romance. And those things he*

said...her frown deepened, and unconsciously she began to nibble on berries...that I was cold and unresponsive and
immature...I must not have loved him.
Sighing, Gwen picked more berries and ate
them, one by one. If I had loved him, I'd have
wanted him to make love to me.

I'm not cold, she thought. I'm not unresponsive. Look at the way I responded to
Luke! She froze with a berry halfway to her
mouth. Her cheeks filled with color. That was
different, she assured herself quickly. Entirely different. She popped the berry into her
mouth. That was simply physical, it had
nothing to do with emotion. Chemistry, that's
all. Why, it's practically scientific.

She speculated on the possibility of seducing Luke. She could flirt and tease and drive
him to the point of distraction, make him fall
in love with her and then cast him off when all
danger to Anabelle was past. It can't be too
difficult, she decided. I've seen lots of the
models twist men around their fingers. She
looked down at her own and noted they were
stained with berry juice.

"Looks as though you've just been booked
by the FBI."

Whirling, Gwen stared at Luke as he leaned back comfortably against a thick cypress. Again he wore jeans and a tee shirt, both faded and well worn. His eyes seemed to take their color from the sky and were more gray now than blue. Gwen's heart hammered at the base of her throat.

"Must you continually sneak up on me?" she snapped. Annoyed with the immediate response of her body to his presence, she spoke heatedly. "You have the most annoying habit of being where you're not wanted."

"Did you know you become more the southern belle when you're in a temper?" Luke asked with an easy, unperturbed smile. "Your vowels flow quite beautifully."

Gwen's breath came out in a frustrated huff. "What do you want?" she demanded.

"To help you pick berries. Though it seems you're doing more eating than picking."

It trembled on her tongue to tell him that she didn't need or want his help. Abruptly, she remembered her resolve to wind him around her berry-stained finger. Carefully she smoothed the frown from between her brows and coaxed her mouth into a charming smile. "How sweet of you."

Luke raised a quizzical eyebrow at her change of tone. "I'm notoriously sweet," he said dryly. "Didn't you know?"

"We don't know each other well, do we?" Gwen smiled and held out the bucket. "At least, not yet."

Slowly, Luke straightened from his stance and moved to join her. He accepted the bucket while keeping his eyes fastened on hers. Determinedly, Gwen kept her own level and unconcerned. She found it difficult to breathe with him so close. "How is your book going?" she asked, hoping to divert him while she regained control of her respiratory system.

"Well enough." He watched as she began to tug berries off the bush again.

"I'm sure it must be fascinating." Gwen slid her eyes up to his in a manner she hoped was provocative and exciting. "I hope you won't think me a bore if I confess I'm quite a fan of yours. I have all your books." This part was easier because it was true.

"It's never a bore to know one's work is appreciated."

Emboldened, Gwen laid her hand on his on the handle of the bucket. Something flashed in his eyes, and her courage fled. Quickly slipping the bucket from his hold, she began to pick berries with renewed interest while cursing her lack of bravery.

"How do you like living in New York?" Luke asked as he began to add to the gradually filling bucket.

"New York?" Gwen cleared her head with a quick mental shake. Resolutely, she picked up the strings of her plan again. "It's very exciting—such a sensual city, don't you think?" Gwen lifted a berry to Luke's lips. She hoped her smile was invitingly alluring, and wished she had thought to practice in a mirror.

Luke opened his mouth to accept her offering. His tongue whispered along the tips of her fingers. Gwen felt them tremble. It took every ounce of will power not to snatch her hand away. "Do you—do you like New York?" Her voice was curiously husky as she began to pull berries again. The tone was uncontrived and by far the most enticing of her tactics.

"Sometimes," Luke answered, then brushed the hair away from her neck.

Moistening her lips, Gwen inched away. "I suppose you live in Louisiana."

"No, I have a place near Carmel, at the beach. What marvellously soft hair you have," he murmured, running his hand through it.

"The beach," Gwen repeated, swallowing. "It must be wonderful. I've—I've never seen the Pacific."

"It can be very wild, very dangerous," Luke said softly before his lips brushed the curve of Gwen's neck.

There was a small, strangled sound from Gwen's throat. She moved further away and fought to keep up a casual front. "I've seen pictures, of course, and movies, but I expect it's quite different to actually see it. I'm sure it's a wonderful place to write."

"Among other things." From behind, Luke dropped his hands to her hips as he caught the lobe of her ear between his teeth. For a moment, Gwen could only lean back against him. Abruptly she stiffened, straightened, and put a few precious inches between them.

"You know," she began, completely abandoning her plans to seduce him, "I believe we have enough." As she turned around, her breasts brushed against his chest. She began to back up, stammering. "Tillie won't want to make more than two—two pies, and there's plenty here for that." Her eyes were wide and terrified.

Luke moved forward. "Then we won't have to waste any more time picking berries, will we?" The insinuation was clear.

"No, well . . ." Her eyes clung helplessly to his as she continued to back up. "Well, I'll just take these in to Tillie. She'll be waiting."

He was still advancing, slowly. Just as Gwen decided to abandon her dignity and run, she stepped backward into empty space. With a sharp cry, she made a desperate grab for Luke's hand. He plucked the bucket from her as she tumbled into the stream.

"Wouldn't want to lose the berries," he explained as Gwen surfaced, coughing and sputtering. "How's the water?"

"Oh!" After beating the surface of the water violently with her fists, Gwen struggled to her feet. "You did that on purpose!" Her hair was plastered to her face, and impatiently she pushed it out of her eyes.

"Did what?" Luke grinned, appreciating the way her clothes clung to her curves.

"Pushed me in." She took two sloshing steps toward the bank.

"My dear Gwenivere," Luke said in a reasonable tone. "I never laid a hand on you."

"Exactly." She kicked at the water in fury. "It's precisely the same thing."

"I suppose it might be from your point of view," he agreed. "But then, you were getting in over your head in any case. Consider the dunking the lesser of two evils. By the way, you have a lily pad on your..." His pause for the sake of delicacy was belied by the gleam in his eyes.

Flushing with embarrassment and fury, Gwen swiped a hand across her bottom. "As I said before, you are no gentleman."

Luke roared with laughter. "Why, Miss Gwenivere, ma'am, your opinion devastates me." His drawl was mocking, his bow low.

"At least," she began with a regal sniff, "you could help me out of this mess."

"Of course." With a show of gallantry, Luke set down the bucket and reached for Gwen's hand. Her wet shoes slid on the slippery bank. To help balance her, he offered his other hand. Just as she reached the top edge, Gwen threw all her weight backward, tumbling them both into the water. This time Gwen surfaced convulsed with laughter.

As she stood, she watched him rise from the water and free his eyes of wet hair with a jerk of his head. Laughter blocked her speech. In silence, Luke watched as the sounds of her uninhibited mirth filled the air.

"How's the water?" she managed to get out before dissolving into fresh peals of laughter. Though she covered her mouth with both hands, it continued to escape and dance on the air. A quick hoot of laughter emerged as she saw his eyes narrow. He took a step toward her, and she began a strategic retreat. She moved with more speed than grace through the water, kicking it high. Giggles caused her to stumble twice. She scrambled up the slope but before she could rise to her feet, Luke caught her ankle. Pulling himself up onto the grass, he pinned Gwen beneath him.

Breathless, Gwen could still not stop laughing. Water dripped from Luke's hair onto her face, and she shook her head as it tickled her skin. A smile lurked in Luke's eyes as he looked down on her.

"I should have known better, I suppose," he commented. "But you have such an innocent face."

"You don't." Gwen took deep gulps of air in a fruitless effort to control her giggles. "Yours isn't innocent at all."

"Thank you."

Abruptly, the heavens opened and rain fell, warm and wild. "Oh!" Gwen began to push against him. "It's raining."

"So it is," Luke agreed, ignoring her squirms. "We might get wet."

The absurdity of his statement struck her suddenly. After staring up at him a moment, Gwen began to laugh again. It was a young sound, appealing and free. Gradually, Luke's expression sobered. In his eyes appeared a desire so clear, so unmistakable, that Gwen's breath caught in her throat. She opened her mouth to speak, but no words came.

"My God," he murmured. "You are exquisite."

His mouth took hers with a raw, desperate hunger. Her mouth was as avid as his, her blood as urgent. Their wet clothing proved no barrier as their bodies fused together in ageless intimacy. His caress was rough, and she revelled in the exquisite pain. The soft moan might have come from either of them. He savaged the vulnerable curve of her neck, tasting, arousing, demanding. His quick, desperate loving took her beyond the edge of reason and into ecstasy.

She felt no fear, only excitement. Here was a passion that sought and found her hidden fires and set them leaping. Rain poured over them unfelt, thunder bellowed unheard. His hands were possessive as they moved over her. Through the clinging dampness of her blouse, his mouth found the tip of her breast. She trembled, murmuring his name as he explored the slender smoothness of her thigh. She wanted him as she had never wanted anyone before.

"Luke?" His name was half question, half invitation.

Lightning flashed and illuminated the bayou. Just as swiftly they were plunged again into gloom.

"We'd better get back," Luke said abruptly, rising. "Your mother will be worried."

Gwen shut her eyes on a sudden stab of hurt. Hurriedly, she scrambled to her feet, avoiding Luke's outstretched hand. She swayed under a dizzying onslaught of emotions. "Gwen," Luke said and took a step toward her.

"No." Her voice shook with the remnants of passion and the beginning of tears. Her eyes as they clung to his were young and devastated. "I must be losing my mind. You had no right," she told him shakily, "you had no right."

"To what?" he demanded roughly and grasped her shoulders. "To begin to make love with you or to stop?" Anger crackled in his voice.

"I wish I'd never seen you! I wish you'd never touched me."

"Oh yes." Temper whipped through Luke's voice as he pulled her close to him again. "I can only say I wish precisely the same, but it's too late now, isn't it?" She had never seen his eyes so lit with fury. "Neither of us seems pleased with what's been started, but perhaps we should finish it." Rain swept around them, slicing through the trees and battering the ground. For a moment, Gwen knew terror. He could take her, she knew, even if she fought him. But worse, she knew he would need no force, no superior strength, after the first touch. Abruptly, he released her and stepped away. "Unless that's what you want," he said softly, "you'd best get out of here."

This time Gwen took his advice. Sobbing convulsively, she darted away among the moss-draped trees. Her one thought—to reach the safety of home.

Chapter Five

The rain had awakened the garden. Twenty-four hours later it was still vibrant. Rose petals dried lazily in the sun while dew clung tenaciously to the undersides of leaves. Without enthusiasm, Gwen moved from bush to bush, selecting firm, young blooms. Since the day before, she had avoided Luke Powers. With a determination born of desperation, she had clung to her mother's company, using Anabelle as both a defense and an offense. If, she had decided, *she* was always with Anabelle, Luke could not be. Nor could he take another opportunity to confuse and humiliate Gwen herself.

The basket on her arm was half filled with flowers, but she felt no pleasure in their colors and scents. Something was happening to her—she knew it, felt it, but could not define it. More and more often, she caught her thoughts drifting away from whatever task she was performing. It is, she reflected as she snipped a slender, thorny rose stem with Anabelle's garden shears, as if even my thoughts aren't wholly mine any longer.

When she considered her behavior over the past two days, Gwen was astounded. She had come to warn her mother about her relationship with Luke Powers and instead had found herself responding to him as she had never responded to Michael or any other man. But then, she admitted ruefully, she had never come into contact with a man like Luke Powers. There was a basically sensual aura about him despite his outward calm. She felt that he, like the bayou, hid much below the surface. Gwen was forced to admit that she had no guidelines for dealing with such a man. Worse, he had kindled in her a hitherto buried part of her nature.

She had always thought her life and her needs simple. But suddenly, the quiet dreams inside her had risen to the surface. She was no longer the uncomplicated, controlled woman she had thought herself to be. The somewhat volatile temper she possessed had always been manageable, but in just two days the reins of restraint had slipped through her fingers.

His fault, Gwen grumbled to herself as she glared at a pale pink peony. He shouldn't be here—he should be in his beach house in California. If he were in California, perhaps battling an earthquake or hurricane, I'd be having a nice, uncomplicated visit with Mama. Instead he's here, insinuating himself into my life and making me feel...Gwen paused a moment and bit her lip. How does he make me feel? she thought. With a sigh, she let her gaze wander over the variety of colors and hues in the garden. I'm not sure how he makes me feel. He frightens me. The knowledge came to her swiftly, and her eyes reflected her surprise. Yes, he frightens me, though I'm not altogether sure why. It's not as if I thought he'd hurt me physically, he's not that sort of man, but still...Shaking her head, Gwen moved slowly down the walkway, digesting the new thought. He's a man who controls people and situations so naturally you're hardly aware you've been controlled.

Unconsciously, Gwen lifted her finger and ran it along her bottom lip. Vividly she remembered the feel of his mouth on hers. Its touch had ranged from gentle and coaxing to urgent and demanding, but the power over her had been the same. It was true—there was something exhilarating about fencing with him, like standing on the bow of a ship in a storm. But no matter how adventurous she might be, Gwen was forced to concede that there was one level on which she could not win. When she was in his arms, it was not surrender she felt but passion for passion, need for need. Discovering this new facet of herself was perhaps the most disturbing knowledge of all.

I won't give up. Gwen lifted her chin and straightened her shoulders. *I won't let him intimidate me or dominate my thoughts any longer.* Her eyes glittered with challenge. *Luke Powers won't control me. He'll find out that Gwen Lacrosse is perfectly capable of taking care of herself and her mother.*

"Just a minute longer." Bradley Stapleton held up a pencil briefly, then continued to scrawl with it on an artist's pad. He sat cross-legged in the middle of the walkway, his feet sandled, wearing paint-spattered carpenter's pants, a checked sport shirt unbuttoned over his thin chest and a beige fisherman's cap on his head. Surprised and intrigued, Gwen stopped in her tracks.

"Wonderful!" With surprising agility, Bradley unfolded himself and rose. His eyes smiled with genuine pleasure as he strolled over to Gwen. "I knew you'd be a good subject, but I didn't dare hope you'd be spectacular. Just look at this range of emotions!" he commanded as he flipped back several pages in his pad.

Gwen's initial amusement altered to astonishment. That the pencil sketches were exceptionally good was obvious, but it was not his talent as much as the content of the sketches that surprised her. She saw a woman with loose, curling hair and a coltish slenderness. There was a vulnerability she had never perceived in herself. As Gwen turned the pages, she saw herself dreaming, pouting, thinking and glaring. There was something disturbing about seeing her feelings of the past half hour so clearly defined. She lifted her eyes to the artist.

"They're fabulous," she told him. Bradley's face crinkled into a grin. "Bradley," she searched for the right words. "Am I really...so, well,...artless as it seems here?"

She looked back down at the sketches with a mixture of conflicting emotions. "What I mean is, are my thoughts, my feelings so blatantly obvious? Am I so transparent?"

"That's precisely what makes you such a good model," Bradley said. "Your face is so expressive."

"But—" With a gesture of frustration, Gwen ran a hand through her hair. "Do they always show? Are they always there for people to examine? I feel defenseless and, well, naked somehow."

Bradley gave her a sympathetic smile and patted her cheek with his long, bony fingers. "You have an honest face, Gwen, but if it worries you, remember that most people don't see past the shape of a nose or the color of eyes. People are usually too busy with their own thoughts to notice someone else's."

"Yet you certainly did," Gwen replied, but she felt more comfortable.

"It's my business."

"Yes." With a smile, Gwen began flipping through the pages again. "You're very good..." She stopped, speechless as the pad fell open to a sketch of Luke.

It was a simple sketch of him sitting on the rail of the veranda. He was dressed casually, and his hair was tousled as though he had been working. Bradley had captured the strength and intelligence in his face, as well as the sensual quality she had not expected another man to notice. But it was Luke's eyes, which seemed to lock onto hers, that impressed her. The artist had caught the strange melding of serenity and power that she had felt in them. Gwen was conscious of an odd quickening of her breath. Irresistibly, she was drawn to the picture just as she was drawn to the man.

"I'm rather pleased with it." Gwen heard Bradley's voice and realized with a jolt that he had been speaking for several seconds.

"It's very good," she murmured. "You understand him." She was unaware of the wistfulness and touch of envy in her voice.

After a brief, speculative glance at her lowered head, Bradley nodded. "To an extent, I suppose. I understand he's a complicated man. In some ways, he's much like you."

"Me?" Genuinely shocked, Gwen lifted her eyes.

"You're both capable of a wide range of emotions. Not everyone is, you know. The main difference is, he channels his while yours are fully expressed. Will you sit for me?"

"What?" Gwen tried to focus on him again. The question was out of context with the rest of his statement. She shook her head to clear it of the disturbing thoughts his words had aroused in her.

"Will you sit for me?" Bradley repeated patiently. "I very much want to do you in oils."

"Yes, of course." She shrugged and conjured up a smile to dispel her own mood. "It sounds like fun."

"You won't think so after a couple of hours of holding a pose," Bradley promised good naturedly. "Come on, we'll get started now before you change your mind." Taking her hand, he pulled her up the walkway.

Several hours later, Gwen clearly understood the truth of Bradley's statement. Posing for a temperamental artist, she discovered, was both exhausting and demanding. Her face had been sketched from a dozen angles while she stood or sat or twisted in accor-

dance with his commands. She began to feel
more sympathy for the models at *Style*.

She had been amused at first when Bradley
rooted through her wardrobe in search of at-
tire suitable to sitting for the portrait. When
he selected a thin white silk robe, she had
taken what she considered a firm stand
against his choice. He ignored her objections
and, to her amazement, Gwen found herself
doing exactly as he instructed.

Now, tired and alone, Gwen stretched out
on her bed and relaxed her muscles. A smile
lurked at the corners of her mouth as she recalled how Bradley had gently steamrolled
her. Any embarrassment she had felt about
wearing only the robe while he studied her or
moved her this way and that had been swiftly
eradicated. She might as easily have been an
interesting tree or a fruit bowl. He had not
been interested in the body beneath the robe
but in the way the material draped.

I don't have to worry about fending off a
passionate attack, Gwen reflected as she shut
her eyes, only about stiffening joints. With a
deep sigh, she snuggled into the pillow.

Her dreams were confused. She dreamed
she was roaming through the bayou picking

roses and blueberries. As she passed through a clearing, she saw Luke chopping down a thick, heavy tree. The sound of the axe was like thunder. The tree fell soundlessly at her feet. As Luke watched, she walked to him and melted into his arms. For an instant she felt violent joy, then just as suddenly, she found herself hurled into the cool stream.

From behind a curtain of water, Gwen saw Anabelle, a gentle smile on her lips as she offered her hand to Luke. Gwen struggled for the surface but found it just beyond her reach. Abruptly she was standing on the bank with Bradley sitting at her feet sketching. Axe in hand, Luke approached her, but Gwen found her arms and legs had turned to stone. As he walked, he began to change, his features dissolving, his clothing altering.

It was Michael who came to her now, a practical briefcase taking the place of the axe. He shook his head at her stone limbs and reminded her in his precise voice that he had told her she was cold. Gwen tried to shake her head in denial, but her neck had turned to stone as well. When Michael took her by the shoulders and prepared to carry her away, she could only make a small sound of protest.

From a distance, she heard Luke call her name. Michael dropped her, and as her stone limbs shattered, she awoke. Dazed, Gwen stared into blue-gray eyes. "Luke," she murmured, "I'm not cold."

"No." He brushed the hair from her cheek, then let his palm linger. "You're certainly not."

"Kiss me again, I don't want to turn to stone." She made the request petulantly. Amusement touched Luke's mouth as he lowered it to hers.

"Of course not, who could blame you?"

Sighing, Gwen locked her arms around his neck and enjoyed the warm gentleness of the kiss. Her limbs grew warm and fluid, her lips parted and begged for more. The kiss deepened until dream and reality mixed. A sharp stab of desire brought Gwen crashing through the barriers of lingering sleep. She managed a muffled protest against his mouth as she struggled for release. Luke did not immediately set her free but allowed his lips to linger on hers until he had had his fill. Even then, his face remained dangerously close. His mouth was only a sigh away.

"That must've been some dream," he murmured. With easy intimacy, he rubbed his nose against hers. "Women are so irresistibly soft and warm when they've been sleeping."

Cheeks flaming, Gwen managed to struggle up to a sitting position. "You have a nerve," she flared. "What do you mean by coming into my bedroom and molesting me?"

"Take a guess," he invited with a wolfish grin. Her color grew yet deeper as she gripped the V of her robe. "Relax," Luke continued. "I didn't come to steal your virtue, I came to wake you for dinner." He ran a fingertip along her jawline. "The rest was your idea."

Indignation stiffened Gwen's spine but muddled her speech. "You—you...I was asleep, and you took advantage..."

"I certainly did," Luke agreed, then pulled her close for a hard, brief kiss. "And we both enjoyed every second of it." He rose gracefully. "White suits you," he commented, his gaze wandering over the soft folds of the robe, "but you might want to change into something a bit less informal for dinner, unless your object is to drive Bradley into a frenzy of desire."

Gwen rose, wrapping the robe more tightly about her. "Don't worry about Bradley," she said icily. "He spent all afternoon sketching me in this robe."

The humor disappeared so swiftly from Luke's face, Gwen wondered if she had imagined its existence. His mouth was grim as he stepped toward her. "What?" The one word vibrated in the room.

"You heard me. I've agreed to let Bradley paint me."

"In that?" Luke's eyes dropped the length of the robe, then returned to her face.

"Yes, what of it?" Gwen tossed her head and turned to walk away from him. The silk of her robe floated around her legs and clung to her hips as she moved. When she reached the window, she turned and leaned back against the sill. Her stance was at once insolent and sensual. "What business is it of yours?"

"Don't play games unless you're prepared to lose," Luke warned softly.

"You're insufferable." The brown of her eyes grew molten.

"And you're a spoiled child."

"I'm not a child," Gwen retorted. "I make my own decisions. If I want to pose for Bradley in this robe or in a suit of armor or in a pair of diamond earrings and nothing else, that's nothing to do with you."

"I'd consider the diamond earrings carefully, Gwen." The soft tone of Luke's voice betrayed his rising temper. "If you try it, I'd have to break all of Bradley's fingers."

His calm promise of violence added fuel to Gwen's fire. "If that isn't typical male stupidity! If something doesn't work, kick it or swear at it! I thought you were more intelligent."

"Did you?" A glimmer of amusement returned to Luke's eyes. Reaching out, he gave her hair a sharp tug. "Too bad you were wrong."

"Men!" she expostulated, lifting her palms and eyes to the ceiling. "You're all the same."

"You speak, of course, from vast personal experience."

The sarcasm in his voice did not escape Gwen. "You're all arrogant, superior, selfish—"

"Beasts?" Luke suggested amiably.

"That'll do," she agreed with a nod.

"Glad to help." Luke sat back on the edge of the bed and watched her. The flickering lights of the setting sun accentuated the hollows and shadows of her face.

"You always think you know best and that women are too muddleheaded to decide things for themselves. All you do is give orders, orders, orders, and when you don't get your own way, you shout or sulk or worse, patronize. I hate, loathe and despise being patronized!" Balling her hands into fists, Gwen thrust them into the pockets of her robe. "I don't like being told I'm cute in a tone of voice that means I'm stupid. I don't like being patted on the head like a puppy who can't learn to fetch. Then, after you've finished insulting my intelligence, you want to breathe all over me. Of course, I should be grateful for the attention because I'm such a sweet little simpleton." Unable to prevent herself any longer, Gwen gave the bedpost a hard slap. "I am not," she began, and her voice was low with fury, "I am *not* cold and unresponsive and sexually immature."

"Good Lord, child." Gwen, jolted by Luke's voice, blinked as she refocused on him. "What idiot ever told you that you were?"

Gwen stared at Luke in frozen silence.

"Your opinion of men obviously comes from the same source," he continued. "Your Michael must have been really convincing." Embarrassed, Gwen shrugged and turned back to the window. "Were you in love with him?"

The question caught her so off balance that she answered automatically. "No, but I thought I was, so it amounts to the same thing, I imagine."

"Bounced around a bit, were you?" His tone was surprisingly gentle as were the hands that descended to her shoulders.

"Oh, please." Quickly, Gwen moved away as she felt a strange, sweet ache. "Don't be kind to me. I can't fight you if you're kind."

"Is that what you want to do?" Luke took her shoulders firmly now and turned her around to face him. "Do you want to fight?" His eyes dropped to her lips. Gwen began to tremble.

"I think it's better if we do." Her voice was suddenly breathless. "I think fighting with you is safer."

"Safer than what?" he inquired. He smiled, a quick, flashing movement that was both charming and seductive. The room grew dim in the dusk, silhouetting them in the magic light of a dying day. "You are beautiful," he murmured, sliding his hand along the slope of her shoulders until his fingers traced her throat.

Mesmerized, Gwen stared up at him. "No, I—I'm not. My mouth's too wide, and my chin's pointed."

"Of course," Luke agreed as he drew her closer. "I see it now, you're quite an ugly little thing. It's a pity to waste velvet eyes and silken skin on such an unfortunate-looking creature."

"Please." Gwen turned her head, and his mouth brushed her cheek rather than her lips. "Don't kiss me. It confuses me—I don't know what to do."

"On the contrary, you seem to know precisely what to do."

"Luke, please." She caught her breath. "Please, when you kiss me, I forget everything, and I only want you to kiss me again."

"I'll be happy to do so."

"No, don't." Gwen pushed away and looked at him with huge, pleading eyes. "I'm frightened."

He studied her with quiet intensity. He watched her lip tremble, her teeth digging into it to halt the movement. The pulse in her neck throbbed under his palm. Letting out a long breath, he stepped back and slipped his hands into his pockets. His look was thoughtful. "I wonder, if I make love to you, would you lose that appealing air of innocence?"

"I'm not going to let you make love to me." Even to herself, Gwen's voice sounded shaky and unsure.

"Gwen, you're much too honest to make a statement like that, let alone believe it yourself." Luke turned and walked to the door. "I'll tell Anabelle you'll be down in a few minutes."

He closed the door behind him, and Gwen was left alone with her thoughts in the darkening room.

Chapter Six

Gwen endured Bradley's sketching for nearly an hour. His eyes were much sharper in his plain, harmless face than she had originally thought. And, she had discovered, he was a quiet tyrant. Once she had agreed to pose for him, he had taken over with mild, but inescapable efficiency. He placed her on a white wrought-iron chair in the heart of the garden.

The morning was heavy and warm, with a hint of rain hovering despite the sunshine. A dragonfly darted past, zooming over a rose bush to her right. Gwen turned her head to watch its flight.

"Don't do that!" Bradley's beautifully modulated voice made Gwen guiltily jerk her head back. "I'm only sketching your face today," he reminded her. She murmured something unintelligible that had him smiling. "Now I understand why you work behind the scenes at *Style* and not in front of the camera." His pencil paused in midair. "You've never learned how to sit still!"

"I always feel as though I should be doing something," Gwen admitted. "How does anyone ever just sit like this? I had no idea how difficult it was."

"Where's your Southern languor?" Bradley asked, sketching in a stray wisp of hair. She would sit more quietly if he kept up a conversation, he decided, even though he did not particularly care for splitting his concentration between sketching and talking.

"Oh, I don't think I ever had it," Gwen told him. She brought up her foot to rest on the chair and laced her hands around her knee. Enjoying the heady perfumes of the garden, she took a deep breath. "And living in New York has made it worse. Although..." She paused, looking around her again, though this time remembering to move only her eyes. "There is something peaceful here, isn't there? I'm discovering how much I've missed that."

"Is your work very demanding?" Bradley asked, perfecting the line of her chin with a dash of his pencil.

"Hmm." Gwen shrugged and longed to take a good stretch. "There's always some deadline that no one could possibly meet that, of course, we meet. Then there are the models and photographers who need their artistic egos soothed—"

"Are you good at soothing artistic egos?" Bradley narrowed his eyes to find the perspective.

"Surprisingly, yes." She smiled at him. "And I like the challenge of meeting deadlines."

"I've never been good with deadlines," he murmured. "Move your chin, so." He gestured with a fingertip, and Gwen obeyed.

"No, some people aren't, but I have to be. When you're a monthly publication, you have no choice."

For a moment, Gwen fell silent, listening to the hum of bees around the azalea bushes in back of her. Somewhere near the house, a bird sent up a sudden, jubilant song. "Where are you from, Bradley?" she asked at length, turning her eyes back to him. He was a strange man, she thought, with his gangly body and wise eyes.

"Boston." His eyes went briefly to her, then back to his sketch pad. "Turn your head to the right a bit . . . There, good."

"Boston. I should have guessed. Your voice is very . . . elegant." Bradley chuckled. "How did you decide to become an artist?"

"It's my favorite mode of communication. I've always loved sketching. In school my teachers had to confiscate my sketchbooks. And, some people are very impressed when they hear you're an artist."

Gwen laughed. "The last's not a real reason."

"Don't be too sure," Bradley murmured, involved with the curve of her cheek. "I enjoy flattery. Not everyone is as self-sufficient as you."

Forgetting his instructions, Gwen turned to him again. "Is that the way you see me?"

"Sometimes." He lifted a brow and motioned for her to turn away again. For a moment he studied her profile before beginning to draw again. "To be an artist, a good one, without the driving passion to be a great one, suits me perfectly." He smiled at her thoughtful expression. "It wouldn't suit you at all. You haven't the patience for it."

Gwen thought of the brisk, no-nonsense Gwen Lacrosse of *Style* Magazine—a practical, efficient woman who knew her job and did it well, a woman who knew how to handle details and people, who was good at facts and figures. And yet...there was another Gwen Lacrosse who loved old, scented gardens and watched weepy movies on television, who hopped into Hansom cabs in the rain. Michael had been attracted to the first Gwen but despaired of the second. She sighed. Perhaps she had never understood the mixture herself. She had not even questioned it. At least not until she had met Luke Powers.

Luke Powers. She didn't want to think about him. Things were not working out quite the way she had planned in that department. Worse yet, she wasn't at all sure they ever would.

Gwen tilted her head up to the sky. Bradley opened his mouth to remonstrate, then finding a new angle to his liking, continued sketching. The sun lit reddish sparks in her hair. She noticed that the clouds were rolling in from the west. A storm was probably brewing, she thought. It was still far off, hovering, taking its time. She had a feeling that it would strike when least expected. Though the day appeared to be sunny and pleasant, she felt the passion there, just below the surface. The air throbbed with it. In spite of the heat, Gwen shivered involuntarily. Irresistibly, her eyes were drawn to the house and up.

Luke was watching her from the window of his room. She wondered how long he had been there, looking down with that quiet, direct expression that she had come to expect from him. His eyes never wavered as hers met them.

He stared without apology, without embarrassment. For the moment, Gwen found herself compelled to stare back. Even with the distance between them, she could feel the intrusion of his gaze. She stiffened against it.

As if sensing her response, Luke smiled...slowly, arrogantly, never shifting his eyes from hers. Gwen read the challenge in them. She tossed her head before turning away.

Bradley cocked a brow at Gwen's scowling face. "It appears," he said mildly, "that we're done for the day." He rose from his perch on a stone, unexpectedly graceful. "Tomorrow morning, I want you in the robe. I've a pretty good idea on the pose I want. I'm going in to see if I can charm Tillie out of a piece of that chocolate cake. Want some?''

Gwen smiled and shook her head. "No, it's a bit close to lunch for me. I think I'll give Mama a hand and do some weeding." She glanced down at the petunia bed. "She seems to be neglecting it a bit.''

"Busy lady," Bradley said, and sticking the pencil behind his ear, sauntered down the path.

Busy lady? Gwen frowned after him. Her mother did not seem preoccupied...but *what* precisely was she doing? Perhaps it was just her way of intimating to Gwen that she too had a life just as important as Gwen's big city profession. Moving over to the petunia bed, Gwen knelt down and began to tug at stray weeds.

Anabelle had developed a habit of disappearing from time to time—that was something new. Unable to do otherwise, she glanced up at Luke's window again. He was gone. With a scowl, she went back to her weeding.

If only he would leave, she thought, everything would be fine. Her mother was a soft, gentle creature who trusted everyone. She simply had no defenses against a man like Luke Powers. And you do? she mocked herself. Swearing, Gwen tugged and unearthed a hapless petunia.

"Oh!" She stared down at the colorful blossom, foolishly guilty. A shadow fell across her, and she stiffened.

"Something upsetting you?" Luke asked. He crouched down beside her; taking the blossom from her hand, he tucked it behind her ear. Gwen remembered the rose and blushed before she could turn her face away.

"Go away. I'm busy," she said.

"I'm not." His voice was carelessly friendly. "I'll help."

"Don't you have work to do?" She shot him a scornful glance before ripping savagely at another weed.

"Not at the moment." Luke's tone was mild as he felt his way among the flowers. His fingers were surprisingly deft. "The advantage of being self-employed is that you make your own hours—at least most of the time."

"Most of the time?" Gwen queried, curiously overcoming her dislike for this annoying man.

"When it works you're chained to the typewriter and that's that."

"Strange," Gwen mused aloud, forgetting to ignore him. "I can't picture you chained to anything. You seem so free. But it must be difficult putting all those words on paper, making the people inside your head walk and talk and think. Why did you decide to become a writer?"

"Because I have an affection for words," he said.

"And because those people in my head are always scrambling to get out. Now I've answered your question frankly." Luke turned to her as he twirled a blade of grass between his fingers. "It's my turn to ask one. What were you thinking of when you were watching the sky?"

Gwen frowned. She wasn't at all sure she wanted to share her private thoughts with Luke Powers. "That we're in for some rain," she compromised. "Must you watch me that way?"

"Yes."

"You're impossible," she told him crossly.

"You're beautiful." His look was suddenly intense, shooting a quiver up her spine. He cupped her chin before she could turn away. "With the sunlight on your hair and your eyes misty, you were all I have ever dreamed of. I wanted you." His mouth drew closer to hers. His breath fluttered over her skin.

"Don't!" Gwen started to back away, but his fingers on her chin held her steady.

"Not so fast," Luke said softly.

His kiss was surprisingly gentle, brushing her mouth like a butterfly's wing. Instinctively, she parted her lips to receive his probing tongue. With a sigh, she succumbed to the mood of the waiting garden. Her passion had lain sleeping, like the threatened storm behind the layer of soft clouds. She trembled with desire as his fingers carefully traced the planes of her face. They caressed her cheekbones, the line of her jaw, the thick tousle of her hair at her temples, before he kissed her again. His tongue teased and tasted with only the slightest pressure. She gripped his shirt front tightly and moaned his name. Her skin was alive with him. Wanting, needing, she twined her arms around his neck and pulled him against her. Her mouth was avid, seeking.

For one blazing moment, the flame rose and consumed them both, as they embraced in the fragrant morning heat. Then, he had drawn her away, and Gwen was staring up at him, trying to catch her breath.

"No." She shook her head, pressing her hands to her temples as she waited for her thoughts to steady. "No." Before she could turn and flee, Luke had sprung up, grabbing her wrist.

"No what?" His voice was deeper, but still calm.

"This isn't right." The words tumbled out of her as she tried to find reason. "Let me go."

"In a minute." Luke kept his hand on her wrist and stepped toward her. A sweeping gaze took in her frantic color and widened eyes. "You want it, and so do I."

"No, no, I don't!" She shot out with a fierce denial and jerked her arm. Her wrist stayed in his grip.

"I don't remember your protesting too much!" he said mildly. She was annoyed to recognize amusement in his eyes. "Yes, I distinctly recall it was you who took matters to the boiling point."

"All right, all right. You win." She took a breath. "I did. I forgot, that's all."

He smiled. "Forgot what?"

Gwen narrowed her eyes at his amusement. It fanned her temper more than his anger would have. "Forgot that I don't like you," she tossed out. "Now let me go, my memory's back."

Luke laughed a joyous masculine laugh before he pulled Gwen back into his arms. "You tempt me to make you forget again, Gwenivere." He kissed her again, a hard and possessive kiss. It was over almost before it had begun, but her senses were already reeling from it. "Shall we go back to weeding?" he asked pleasantly, as he released her.

She drew herself straight, indignant, furious. "You can go..."

"Gwen!" Anabelle's soft voice cut off Gwen's suggestion. Her mother had drifted into the garden. "Oh, here you are, both of you. How nice."

"Hello Anabelle." Luke gave her an easy smile. "We thought we'd give you a hand with the garden!"

"Oh?" She looked vaguely at her flowers, then her face brightened with a smile. "That's sweet, I'm sure I haven't been as diligent as I should be, but . . ." She trailed off watching a bee swoop down on a rosebud. "Perhaps we can all get back to this later. Tillie's got lunch ready and insists on serving right away. It's her afternoon off, you know." She turned her smile on Gwen. "You'd better wash your hands, dear," she looked anxiously at Gwen, "and perhaps you should stay out of the sun for awhile, you're a bit flushed."

Gwen could feel Luke grin without looking at him. "You're probably right," she mumbled. Detestable man! Why did he always succeed in confusing her?

Unaware of the fires raging in her daughter, Anabelle smilingly laid a hand on Gwen's cheek, but whatever she planned to say was distracted by the drone of a furry bee. "My, my," she said, watching it swoop greedily down on an azalea blossom. "He's certainly a big one." Having forgotten Tillie's instructions, she glanced back up at Gwen. "You were sitting for Bradley this morning, weren't you, dear?''

"Yes." Gwen made a face. "For almost two hours."

"Isn't that exciting?" Anabelle glanced up at Luke for his confirmation, then continued before he could comment. "A portrait painted by a real artist! I can hardly wait to see it when it's all finished! Why, I'll have to buy it, I suppose." Her blue eyes brightened. "Perhaps I'll hang it right over the mantel in the parlor. That is . . ." Another thought intruded, and she stopped her planning and re-arranging to look at her daughter. "Unless you want it for you and your Michael."

"He isn't *my* Michael, Mama, I told you." Gwen stuck her hands in her pockets, wishing Luke would say something instead of simply watching her with those cool blue-gray eyes. Why was it never possible to tell what he was thinking? "And in any case, he'd never buy a painting from an unknown. He wouldn't be assured of the investment value," she added. She was sorry that a note of rancor slipped into her voice.

Luke's eyes remained cool, but Gwen saw his brow lift fractionally. He doesn't miss anything, she thought with a stab of resentment. Turning, she began to pull loose petals from an overbloomed rose.

"Oh, but surely, if it were a portrait of you," Anabelle began. Observing her daughter's expression, she hastily changed her course. "I'm sure it's going to be just beautiful," she said brightly. She turned to Luke. "Don't you think so, Luke?"

"Undoubtedly," he agreed as Gwen gave the rose her fiercest attention. "Bradley has the raw material to work with. That is..." He paused, and unable to resist, Gwen looked over her shoulder to meet his eyes again. "If Gwenivere manages to hold still until it's finished."

Gwen's spine stiffened at the amusement in his voice, but before she could retort, Anabelle laughed gaily. "Oh yes, Gwen's a ball of fire, I declare," she emoted. "Even as a youngster, flitting here and there, quicker than a minute. Why I'd have to nearly chain her to a chair to braid her hair." She smiled in maternal memory, absently fluffing her own hair. "Then, at the end of the day, or most times long before, it looked as though I had never touched it! And her clothes!" She clucked her tongue and rolled her eyes. "Oh, what a time I used to have with torn knees and ripped seams."

"Mama." Gwen interrupted before Anabelle could launch into another speech on her girlhood. "I'm sure Luke's not interested in the state of my clothes."

He grinned at that, widely, irreverently. Gwen blushed to the roots of her hair. "On the contrary," he said as she groped around for something scathing and dignified to say. "I'm extremely interested." His eyes softened as he smiled at Anabelle. "It's all grist for my mill—just the sort of background material a writer needs."

"Why yes, I suppose so." Gwen saw that her mother found this extremely profound. Anabelle lapsed into silence again, dreaming off into middle distance. Luke grinned at Gwen over her head.

"And I've always had a fondness for little girls," he told her. "Particularly ones whose braids won't stay tied, and who regularly scrape their knees." He glanced down, letting his eyes run over Gwen's French-cut tee shirt and cinnamon colored shorts. "I imagine over the years Anabelle was pretty busy administering first aid." His eyes traveled up on the same slow, casual journey before meeting hers.

"I didn't make a habit of falling down," Gwen began, feeling ridiculous.

Anabelle came out of her trance for a moment. "Oh, yes." She picked up on Luke's comment. "I don't think a day went by when I wasn't patching up some hurt. A fishhook in your hand one day..." She shuddered at the memory. "And a lump the size of a goose egg on your forehead the next. It was always one thing or another."

"Mama." Gwen crushed what was left of the rose between her fingers. "You make it sound as if I had been a walking disaster."

"You were just spirited, darling." Anabelle frowned a bit at the damaged rose, but made no comment. "Though there were times, I admit, I wasn't certain you'd live to grow up. But, of course, you have, so I probably shouldn't have worried so much."

"Mama." Gwen was suddenly touched. How difficult it must have been, she reflected, for such a young, dreamy woman to raise a lively youngster all on her own! How many sacrifices Anabelle must have made that

Gwen had never even considered. Stepping over, Gwen put her hands on Anabelle's soft rounded shoulders. "I love you, and I'm terribly glad you're my mother."

With a sound of surprised pleasure, Anabelle framed Gwen's face and kissed both her cheeks. "What a sweet thing to hear, and from a grown daughter, too." She gave Gwen a quick, fragrant hug.

Over her mother's shoulder, Gwen saw that Luke was still watching them. His direct intensity made her feel self-conscious.

How do I really feel about him? she asked herself. And how can I feel anything, anything at all when the woman I love most in the world stands between us? She felt trapped, and something of her panic showed in her eyes.

Luke tilted his head. "You're very fortunate, Anabelle." He spoke to the mother, though his eyes remained on the daughter. "Love is very precious."

"Yes." She kissed Gwen's cheek again, then linked her arm through her daughter's. "I'm in a festive mood," she told them both, glowing. "I think we should be daring and have some wine with lunch." Her eyes widened. "*Lunch!* Oh, dear, Tillie will be furious! I completely forgot." She rested a hand against her heart as if to calm it. "I'll go smooth things along. Give me a minute." She assumed a business-like air. "Then come right in. And see that you make a fuss over whatever she's fixed. We don't want to hurt her feelings any more than we have." She gave the final instructions as she swept back up the path and disappeared.

Gwen started to follow. Luke neatly cut off her retreat by taking her hand. "You'd better let her play diplomat first," he told her.

Gwen swung around to face him. "I don't want to be here with you."

Luke lifted a brow, letting his eyes play over her face. "Why not? I can't imagine more attractive circumstances. This lovely garden...A beautiful day...Tell me something," he continued, interrupting whatever retort she might have made. Casually, he tangled the fingers of his other hand in her hair. "What were you thinking of when you hugged your mother and looked at me?"

"That's none of your business." Gwen jerked her head, trying to free her hair from his curious fingers.

"Really?" He lifted and stroked a straying lock of her hair. Somewhere in the distant west, she heard the first rumbles of thunder. "I had the impression whatever was going through your mind at that moment was very much my business." He brought his eyes back down to hers and held them steady. "Why do you suppose I did?"

"I haven't the faintest idea," Gwen returned coolly. "Probably an author's overheated imagination."

Luke's smile moved slowly, touching his eyes seconds before it touched his lips. "I don't think so, Gwen. I prefer thinking of it as a writer's intuition."

"Or a man's over-inflated ego," she shot back, lifting her hand to her hair in an attempt to remove his exploring fingers. "Would you stop that!" she demanded, trying to ignore the dancing of nerves at the back of her neck.

"Or a man's sensitivity to a woman," he countered, bringing her hand to his lips. He kissed her fingers one at a time until she regained the presence of mind to try to jerk free. Instead of releasing her, Luke simply laced fingers with hers. They stood, joined as carelessly as schoolchildren while she frowned at him. The thunder came again, closer. "Sensitive enough to know when a woman who is attracted to me," he went on lazily, "is not willing to admit it."

Her eyes narrowed. "You're impossibly conceited."

"Hopelessly honest," he corrected. "Shall I prove it to you?"

Gwen lifted her chin. "There's nothing to prove." She knew the hopelessness of attempting to pull her hand from his. Casually, she looked past him to the sky. "The clouds are coming in, I don't want to get caught in the rain."

"We've got a minute," he said, without even glancing at the sky. He smiled. "I believe I make you nervous."

"Don't flatter yourself," she tossed back and kept her hands calm in his.

"The pulse in your throat is hammering." His eyes dropped and lingered on it, further increasing its pace. "It's strangely attractive—"

"It always does when I'm annoyed," she said, fighting for poise as the sweep of his eyes from her throat to her face threatened to destroy her composure.

"I like you when you're annoyed. I like to watch the different expressions on your face and to see your eyes darken...but..." He trailed off, slipping his hands to her wrists. "At the moment, I believe it's nerves."

"Believe what you like." It was impossible to prevent her pulse from pounding against his fingers. She tried to calm her rebel blood. "You don't make me the least bit nervous."

"No?" His grin turned wolfish. Gwen braced for a struggle. "A difference of opinion," he observed. "And one I'm tempted to resolve." He drew her closer, letting his eyes rest on her mouth. Gwen knew he was baiting her and held her ground. She said nothing, waiting for him to make his move.

"At the moment, however, I'm starved." Luke grinned, then gave her a quick, unexpected kiss on the nose. "And I'm too much of a coward to risk Tillie's bad temper." He dropped one of her hands, but kept the other companionably linked with his. "Let's eat," he suggested, ignoring Gwen's frown.

Chapter Seven

Gwen noticed several small changes in Anabelle. There was an air of secrecy about her that Gwen found out of character. She disappeared so often, Gwen thought as she seated herself in front of the vintage Steinway in the parlor. She's here one minute and gone the next. And she spends too much time with Luke Powers. There are too many discussions that stop abruptly when I walk in on them. They make me feel like an intruder. With little interest, she began to pick out a melody. The breeze came softly through the window, barely stirring the curtain. The scent of jasmine was elusive, teasing the senses.

I'm jealous, Gwen realized with a jolt of surprise. I expected Mama's undivided attention, and I'm not getting it. With a rueful laugh, Gwen began to play Chopin. Now when have I ever had Mama's undivided attention? She's always had her "visitors," her antiques, her flowers.

Thinking back over childhood memories, Gwen played with absent-minded skill. She had forgotten how soothing the piano was to her. I haven't given myself enough time for this, she reflected. I should take a step back and look at where my life is going. I need to find out what's missing. Her fingers stilled on the last note, which floated quietly through the air and then vanished.

"Lovely," Luke said. "Really lovely."

Gwen suppressed the desire to jump at the sound of his voice. She forced herself to raise her eyes and meet his, struggling to keep the color from tinting her cheeks. It was difficult, after what she had said the evening before, to face him. She felt her defenses were shaky, her privacy invaded. He knew more of her now than she wanted him to.

"Thank you," she said politely. "I am, as Mama always said I would be, grateful for the music lessons she forced me to take."

"Forced?" To Gwen's consternation, Luke sat down on the stool beside her.

"As only she can." Gwen relieved a portion of her tension by giving her attention to another melody. "With quiet, unarguable insistence."

"Ah." Luke nodded in agreement. "And you didn't want to study piano?"

"No, I wanted to study crawfishing." She was stunned when he began to play along with her, picking out the melody on the treble keys. "I didn't know you played." The utter disbelief in her voice brought on his laugh.

"Believe it or not, I, too, had a mother." He gave Gwen his swift, conspiratorial grin. "I wanted to study rock skipping."

Totally disarmed, Gwen smiled back at him. Something passed between them. It was as strong and as real as the passion that had flared with their kiss, as gentle and soothing as the music drifting from the keys.

"Isn't that sweet." Anabelle stood in the doorway and beamed at both of them. "Duets are so charming."

"Mama." Gwen was relieved her voice did not tremble. "I looked for you earlier."

"Did you?" Anabelle smiled. "I'm sorry, dear, I've been busy with . . . this and that," she finished vaguely. "Aren't you sitting for Bradley today?"

"I've already given him his two hours this morning," Gwen answered. "It's lucky for me he wants the early light, or I'd be sitting all day. I thought perhaps you had something you'd like me to do or someplace you'd like me to take you. It's such a lovely day."

"Yes, it is, isn't it?" Anabelle agreed. Her eyes drifted momentarily to Luke's. Abruptly, her cheeks dimpled and her lips curved. "Why, as a matter of fact, darling, there *is* something you could do for me. Oh—" She paused and shook her head. "But it's so much trouble."

"I don't mind," Gwen interrupted, falling into a childhood trap.

"Well, if it really isn't a bother," Anabelle continued, beaming again. "I especially wanted some embroidery thread, very unusual shades, difficult to find, I'm afraid. There's a little shop in the French Market that carries them."

"In New Orleans?" Gwen's eyes widened.

"Oh, it is a bother, isn't it?" Anabelle sighed. "It's not important, dear. Not important at all," she added.

"It's not a bother, Mama," Gwen corrected, smiling at the old ruse. "Besides, I'd like to get into New Orleans while I'm home. I can be a tourist now."

"What a marvelous idea!" Anabelle enthused. "Wouldn't it be fun? Roaming through the *Vieux Carré,* wandering through the shops, listening to the music in Bourbon Street. Oh, and dinner at some lovely gallery restaurant. Yes." She clapped her hands together and glowed. "It's just the thing."

"It sounds perfect." Anabelle's childlike enthusiasm caused Gwen to smile. Shopping, she remembered, had always been Anabelle's favorite pastime. "I can't think of a better way to spend the day."

"Good. It's settled then." She turned to Luke with a pleased smile. "You'll go with Gwen, won't you, dear? It wouldn't do for her to go all alone."

"Alone?" Gwen cut in, confused. "But, Mama, aren't you—?"

"It's such a long drive, too," Anabelle bubbled on. "I'm sure Gwen would love the company."

"No, Mama, I—"

"I'd love to." Luke easily overruled Gwen's objections. He gave Gwen an ironic smile. "I can't think of a better way to spend the day."

"Gwen, dear, I'm so glad you thought of it." The praise was given with a sigh as Anabelle moved over to pat Gwen's cheek.

Looking up into the ingenuous eyes, Gwen felt the familiar sensations of affection and frustration. "I'm very clever," she murmured, moving her lips into a semblance of a smile.

"Yes, of course you are," Anabelle agreed, and gave her a quick, loving hug. "I would change though, darling. It wouldn't do to go into the city in those faded old jeans. Didn't I throw those out when you were fifteen? Yes, I'm sure I did. Well, run along and have fun," she ordered as she began to drift from the room. "I've just so much to do, I can't think of it all."

"Mama." Gwen called after her. Anabelle turned at the door, lifting her brows in acknowledgement. "The thread?"

"Thread?" Anabelle repeated blankly. "Oh, yes, of course. I'll write down the colors and the name of the shop." She shook her head with a self-deprecating smile. "My, my, I'm quite the scatterbrain. I'll go in right now and tell Tillie you won't be here for dinner. She gets so annoyed with me when I forget things. Do change those pants, Gwen,'' she added as she started down the hall.

''I'd hide them,'' Luke suggested confidentially. ''She's liable to throw them out again.''

Rising with what she hoped was dignity, Gwen answered, ''If you'll excuse me?''

''Sure.'' Before she could move away, Luke took her hand in a light but possessive grip. ''I'll meet you out front in twenty minutes. We'll take my car.''

A dozen retorts trembled on Gwen's tongue and were dismissed. ''Certainly. I'll try not to keep you waiting.'' She walked regally from the room.

The weather was perfect for a drive—sunny and cloudless with a light breeze. Gwen had replaced her jeans with a snowy crepe de chine dress. It had a high, lacy neck and pleated bodice, its skirt flowing from a trim, tucked waist. She wore no jewelry. Her hair lay free on her shoulders. Hands primly folded in her lap, she answered Luke's easy conversation with polite, distant monosyllables. I'll get Mama's thread, she determined, have a token tour of the city and drive back as quickly as possible. I will be perfectly polite the entire time.

An hour later, Gwen found that maintaining her aloof sophistication was a difficult task. She had forgotten how much she loved the *Vieux Carré*. It was not just the exquisite iron grillwork balconies, the profusion of flowering plants, the charm of long wooden shutters or buildings that had stood for centuries. It was the subtle magic of the place. The air was soft and seemed freshly washed, its many scents ranging from flowery to spicy to the rich smell of the river.

"Fabulous, isn't it?" Luke asked as they stood on the curb of a street too narrow for anything but pedestrian traffic. "It's the most stable city I know."

"Stable?" Gwen repeated, intrigued enough to turn and face him directly.

"It doesn't change," he explained with a gesture of his hand. "It just continues on." Before she realized his intent, he laced his fingers with hers and began to walk. She tugged and was ignored.

"There's no reason to hold my hand," Gwen told him primly.

"Sure there is," he corrected, giving her a friendly smile. "I like to."

Gwen subsided into silence. Luke's palm was hard, the palm of a man used to doing manual labor. She remembered suddenly the feel of it caressing her throat. He sighed, turned and pulled her hard against him, covering her mouth in an unexpected and dizzying kiss. Gwen had no time to protest or respond before she was drawn away again. Along the crowded street, several people applauded.

Gwen and Luke walked past the many street artists in Jackson Square. They paused briefly to admire the chalk portraits of tourists, the oils of city scenes, and the mysterious studies of the bayous. Gwen was torn between her desire to share her pleasure at returning to the city of her childhood and the feeling that she should ignore the dominating man by her side. She was not here to have a good time, she reminded herself sternly. She was here to do an errand. It was on the tip of her tongue to remind Luke of the purpose of their trip when she saw the magician. He was dressed in black, with spangles and a rakish beret and a flowing moustache.

"Oh, look!" Gwen pointed. "Isn't he wonderful?" She moved closer, unconsciously pulling Luke along by tightening her grip on his hand.

They watched brilliantly colored scarves appear from nowhere, huge bouquets of paper flowers grow from the magician's palm and coins sprout from the ears of onlookers. Two young clowns in whiteface entertained the stragglers by twisting balloons into giraffe and poodle shapes. Some distance away, guitarists sold their songs to passing tourists. Gwen could just hear their close-knit harmony.

Forgetting all her stern resolutions, she turned to grin at Luke. He dropped a bill into the cardboard box that served as the portable cash register for the magician. Reaching out, he pinched her chin between his thumb and forefinger. "I knew it wouldn't last too long."

"What wouldn't?" She brushed the hair from her eyes in a habitual gesture.

"You enjoy things too much to remain cool for long," he told her. "No, now don't do that," he ordered, running a finger down her nose as she frowned. He smiled, then brushed his lips over her fingertips. "Shall we be friends?"

Her hand, already warm from his, grew warmer at the kiss. She knew his charm was practiced, his smile a finely tuned weapon. She forced herself to be cautious.

"I don't know that I'd go as far as that," she replied, studying him with eyes that were warily amused.

"Fellow tourists?" he suggested. His thumb moved gently across her knuckles. "I'll buy you an ice cream cone."

Gwen knew she was losing to the smile and the persuasive voice. "Well..." It would do no harm to enjoy the day. No harm in enjoying the city, the magic...in enjoying him. "Two scoops," she demanded, answering his smile with her own.

They moved at an easy pace through the park, enjoying both shade and sun. All around was the soft, continuous cooing from hundreds of pigeons. They flocked along the ground, flocked when chased by children, sunned atop the statue of Andrew Jackson on a rearing horse. Here and there people sat or slept on curved black benches. A young girl sat in a patch of shade and played softly on a recorder.

They walked along the levee and looked at the brown waters of the Mississippi. Lazy music from calliopes provided a pleasant background as they talked of everything and of nothing. The bells of St. Louis Cathedral chimed the hour. They laughed at the toddler who escaped from his mother and splashed in the cool waters of a fountain.

They walked along Bourbon Street, listening to the tangled, continuous music that poured from open doors. Jazz and country and rock merged into one jumbled, compelling sound. They applauded the old man who danced in the street to the demanding strains of *Tiger Rag*. They listened to the corner saxophone player whose lonely song brought Gwen to tears.

On a gallery overlooking a narrow street surging with people, they ate shrimp gumbo and drank cold dry wine. They lingered over the leisurely meal, watching the sun slowly disappear. Pleasantly weary, Gwen toyed with the remains of her cheesecake and watched the first stars come out. Laughter rose from the street below. When she turned, she found Luke studying her over the rim of his glass.

"Why do you look at me like that?" Her smile was completely relaxed as she rested her chin on her palm.

"A remarkably foolish question," Luke answered as he set down his glass. "Why do you think?"

"I don't know." She took a deep breath. The scent of the city assailed her senses. "No one's ever looked at me quite the way you do. You can tell too much about people. It's not fair. You study them and steal their thoughts. It's not a very comfortable feeling."

Luke smiled, and his fingers were light on the back of her hand.

Gwen lifted an eyebrow, then strategically moved her hand out of reach. "You also have a way of making people say things. Yesterday I..." Gwen hesitated and twisted the stem of her glass between her fingers. "I said things to you I shouldn't have. It's disturbing to know you've revealed your emotions to someone else." She sipped her wine. "Michael always says I'm too open."

"Your emotions are beautiful." Gwen looked up, surprised at the tenderness in his voice. "Michael is a fool."

Quickly she shook her head. "Oh no, he's really quite brilliant and he never does anything foolish. He has an image to maintain. It's just that I was beginning to feel as if I were being molded into his conception of a proper attorney's wife."

"He asked you to marry him?" Luke asked, as he poured wine into both glasses.

"He was sure that I would. He was furious when I didn't jump at the offer." Gwen sighed and made a restless movement with her shoulders. "I kept seeing a long, narrow tunnel, very straight, no curves, no detours, no surprises. I guess I developed claustrophobia." She made a frustrated sound, wrinkling her nose. "There, you've done it again."

"I have?" He smiled as he leaned back in his seat. Moonlight spilled over her hair.

"I'm telling you things...things I've barely told myself. You always manage to find out what's in a person's mind, but you keep your own thoughts all tidy and tucked away."

"I put them in print," he corrected. "For anyone who cares to read them."

"Yes," she said slowly. "But how does one know if they're your real thoughts? Your books are interesting, but how do I know who you really are?"

"Do you want to?" There was a soft challenge in his voice.

Gwen hesitated, but the answer was already moving to her lips. "Yes, I do."

"But you're not quite sure." He rose, then held out his hand to her. "The wine's made you sleepy," he said, looking down into her heavy eyes. "Shall I take you home?"

"No." Gwen shook her head. "No, not yet." She slipped her hand back into his.

Luke drove down the magnolia-lined lane. The scent of the night was delicate, mixing with the fragrance of the woman who slept on his shoulder. After stopping the car, he turned his head and looked down at her. Gwen's mouth was soft and vulnerable in sleep. There was a moment's hesitation before he lifted her chin and drew away from her.

"Gwen." He moved his thumb gently over her lips. She gave a soft, pleased sigh. "Gwen," he said again with more firmness. Her lashes fluttered and opened. "We're home." He massaged her shoulders lightly, and she stretched under his hands.

"Did I fall asleep?" Her eyes were huge and dark as she smiled at him. "I didn't mean to."

"It's late."

"I know." She smiled sleepily. "I had fun. Thank you." On impulse, she bent forward and brushed her lips over his. His fingers tightened on her shoulders as he pulled away from her sharply. Gwen blinked in confusion. "Luke?"

"I have my limits," he said tersely. He made a quick, impatient sound as her face registered consternation. "I told you once women are very soft and warm when they've been sleeping. I have a weakness for soft, warm women."

"I didn't mean to fall asleep," she murmured as his hand slipped around to cradle the back of her neck. Her head felt light, her limbs heavy.

A cloud drifted over the moon. The light shifted, dimmed and glowed again. He was watching her, studying each feature with absorption. She could feel his fingers on the base of her neck. They were hard and long, their strength obvious even in the gentle touch. She whispered, "What do you want?"

In answer, he bent slowly toward her. His mouth was easy, teasing the corners of hers, drifting to her closed lids, exploring the hollows of her cheeks. Passion lay simmering beneath the surface as he began to caress her body with slow, patient hands. He traced her parted lips with the tip of his tongue. "Beautiful," he murmured, moving his mouth to her ear. She shivered with pleasure as his thumb lingered on the point of her breast. "When I touch you, I feel your body melt under my hands." He met her mouth with a long, tender kiss. "What do I want?" he answered as he tasted the heated skin of her throat. "What I want more than anything at this moment is to make love with you. I want to take you slowly, until I know all of you."

She felt her body growing fluid, and her will flowed with it. "Will you make love with me?" She heard herself ask, heard the tone that was request rather than question. Luke's mouth paused on her skin. Slowly he tightened his grip on her hair, then drew her head back until their eyes met. For a moment, they hung suspended in silence with only the echo of her voice between them.

"No." His answer was cool and quick as a slap. Gwen jerked away from it and him and fumbled with the handle of the door. She stumbled out of the car, but before she could escape into the house, Luke captured her arms in a firm grip. "Wait a minute."

Shaking her head, Gwen pushed against him. "No, I want to go in. I didn't know what I was saying. It was crazy."

"You knew exactly what you were saying," Luke corrected, tightening his grasp.

Gwen wanted to deny it, but found it impossible. She had wanted him, she knew she still wanted him. "All right, I knew what I was saying. Now will you let me go?"

"I won't apologize for touching you," he said.

"I'm not asking for apologies, Luke," she told him evenly. "I'm simply asking for my freedom." She realized uncomfortably that it was not freedom from his arms that she meant, but freedom from the power he held over her. The struggle inside her was reflected briefly in her face. Luke's frown deepened before he released her arms. "Thank you," she said.

She walked quickly inside the house before he could say another word.

Chapter Eight

A yellow butterfly fluttered delicately over a pot of white impatiens. From the veranda, Gwen watched its dance until it skimmed away, light as the air. Sitting in the white porch rocker, dressed in a yellow sundress, Anabelle looked as fragile as the butterfly. Gwen studied her mother's soft pink cheeks and gentle blue eyes. Anabelle's small hands were busy with the domestic task of shelling peas, but her eyes were, as always, dreamy. Watching her, Gwen was swamped with waves of love and helplessness.

Who am I? she demanded of herself. Who am I to advise anyone on men? For a moment, Gwen wished desperately that she could seek from Anabelle advice for herself. Her own emotions were chaotic. She was terrified that her own feelings for Luke were approaching a dangerous level. Falling in love with a man like Luke was courting disaster. And yet, Gwen wondered unhappily, is it really possible for the mind to control the heart? In this case it must...there's no choice. I have to forget about last night. The sigh escaped before she could stop it. Priorities, she reminded herself. Gwen watched a bumblebee dive into a cluster of wisteria, then took a deep breath and turned to Anabelle. "Mama." Anabelle went on shelling peas, a misty smile on her lips. "Mama," Gwen repeated more sharply, placing a hand over her mother's.

"Oh, yes dear?" Anabelle looked up with the open, expectant look of a child. "Did you say something?"

For an instant, Gwen teetered on the brink, then plunged. "Mama, don't you think twelve years is a terribly big gap?"

Gravely, Anabelle considered. "Why, I suppose it could be, Gwenivere, but then, as you grow older, twelve years is hardly any time at all." Her momentary seriousness vanished with a fresh smile. "Why, it seems like yesterday that you were twelve years old. I remember quite clearly when you fell out of that old cypress in the backyard and broke your arm. Such a brave child . . ." She began shelling peas again. "Never shed a tear. I cried enough for both of us, though."

"But Mama." Valiantly Gwen tried to keep Anabelle's thoughts from straying. "Twelve years, when you're speaking of a man and a woman...." Anabelle failed to respond to the prompting, only nodding to indicate she was listening. "The age difference, Mama," Gwen blurted out. "Isn't twelve years a terribly wide age gap?"

"Sally Deumont's girls are nearly twelve years apart," Anabelle stated with another series of nods. "I suppose having children that far apart has its drawbacks."

"No, Mama." Gwen ran both hands through her hair.

"And its advantages, certainly," Anabelle soothed, not wanting to be critical of an old friend.

"No, Mama, I don't mean that at all. I'm speaking of men and women...of relationships. Romantic relationships."

"Oh!" Anabelle blinked in surprise and smiled. "That's a different matter altogether, isn't it?" Gwen resisted grinding her teeth as her mother continued to shell peas for a moment in silence. "I'm surprised," Anabelle said at length, giving Gwen a look of gentle curiosity. "I'm surprised you would think that age and love had anything to do with each other. I've always thought of the heart as ageless."

The words caused Gwen to falter a moment. Slowly she leaned forward and took both her mother's hands in hers. "Mama, don't you think, sometimes, that love can blind people to what's right for them? Don't people often put themselves into a position where getting hurt is the only possible outcome?"

"Yes, of course." Anabelle shook her head as if startled by the question. "That's part of life. If you never open yourself for pain, you never open yourself for joy. How empty life would be then. This Michael of yours," Anabelle continued with a light of concern in her eyes, "did he hurt you terribly?"

"No." Gwen released her mother's hands and rose to walk the length of the veranda. "No, basically only my pride."

"That can happen by a fall off a horse," Anabelle stated. Abandoning her peas, she moved to join Gwen. "Darling, how young you are." She turned to face her, studying her with rare total concentration. "I sometimes forget that, because you're so much more practical and organized than I am. I suppose I always let you take care of me, much more than I took care of you."

"Oh, no, Mama," Gwen protested, but Anabelle placed a finger on her lips.

"It's true. I never like to look at the unpleasant side of things; I'm afraid I've always let you do that for me. In some ways you matured so quickly, but in others...." Anabelle sighed and slipped an arm around Gwen's waist. "Perhaps at last we've found something I can help you with."

"But, Mama, it's not me...." Gwen began, only to be ignored.

"Did you know I was only eighteen when I first saw your father? I fell instantly, wildly in love." The soft look in Anabelle's eyes halted Gwen's interruption. "Who would have thought his life would be so short? He never even got to see you. I always thought that the greatest tragedy. He would have been so proud to see himself in you." She sighed, then smiled at Gwen. "Ours was a first love, a desperate love, and often I've wondered if it would have withstood all the tests of time. I'll never know." Gwen remained silent, fascinated by a side of her mother she was seeing for the first time. "I learned so many things from that short, crowded marriage. I learned you must always accept love when it's offered, always give it when it's needed. There might not be a second chance. And I know, too, that until your heart's been broken, you never know the full beauty of love."

Gwen watched a squirrel dart across the lawn and scurry up a tree. It was an odd feeling, hearing her mother speak of being in love. She wondered if their relationship had blinded her from seeing Anabelle as a woman with needs and desires. Looking down, Gwen saw the smooth, untroubled skin of a woman at the peak of her beauty. There was still a youthful sweetness in the shape of the mouth, an impossible air of innocence in the eyes. Impulsively, Gwen asked the question that had lurked in her mind for years.

"Mama, why haven't you ever gotten married again?"

"I haven't wanted to," Anabelle answered instantly. She moved away with a swish of her skirts. "At first, I was too much in love with your father's memory, and later I was having too much fun raising you." She plucked a withered fuchsia bloom from a hanging basket and dropped it over the railing of the veranda. "I'm quite good with babies, you know. Later you became more and more independent, so I moved on to the next stage. I've had some admirers." She smiled, pleased with the thought. "I've simply never had the urge to settle down with any of them." In silence, Gwen watched Anabelle move from flower to flower. It occurred to her for the first time that her mother had probably enjoyed love affairs over the past twenty years. She had not been exclusively Gwen's dreamy, gentle mother but Anabelle Lacrosse, a lovely, desirable woman. For one brief moment, Gwen felt ridiculously like an orphan.

I'm being a fool, Gwen told herself, resting her head against the rail post. She's still the same person—I'm the one who's changing. I grew up, but I've kept her locked in a childhood image. It's time I let her out. But I can't bear to see her hurt, and I'm so afraid Luke will leave her wounded. He can't love her, not when he can kiss me the way he does. No.... She closed her eyes. He wants me, but it has nothing to do with his heart. He wants me, but he turned away from me. Why else would he have done that if not for her? A bright flash of jealousy both stunned and shamed her. With a shuddering sigh, she turned to find Anabelle studying her.

"You're not happy," her mother said simply.

"No." Gwen shook her head with the word.

"Confused?"

"Yes." Quickly she swallowed the tears that threatened to come.

"Men do that to us so easily." Anabelle smiled as if the prospect was not altogether unappealing. "Try a rare piece of advice from your mother, darling. Do nothing." With a little laugh, she tossed back a stray wisp of golden hair. "I know how difficult that is for you, but do try. Just let the pieces fall into place around you for a time. Sometimes doing nothing is doing everything."

"Mama." Gwen was forced to smile. "How can something so silly make so much sense?"

"Luke says I've an intuitive understanding." Anabelle replied with a glow of pride.

"He has a way with words," Gwen muttered.

"Tools of the trade." Luke spoke as the screen door swung shut behind him. His eyes met Gwen's. There was something intimate in the glance, something possessive. Even as the stirring began inside her, she lifted her chin in defense. A smile teased his mouth. "Guns primed, Gwenivere?"

"I'm a dead shot," she returned evenly.

"Oh dear." Anabelle moved lightly across the veranda and began to gather her peas. "You didn't tell me you were going hunting. I hope Tillie packed you a lunch."

Luke grinned over her head with such easy boyish charm, Gwen was helpless to resist. Her eyes warmed, and her mouth softened as they shared the intimacy of a joke.

"Actually, I had fishing in mind," Luke countered, keeping his eyes on Gwen's. "I thought I'd walk down to Malon's cabin."

"That's nice." Anabelle straightened and smiled. "Malon still brings up fresh fish," she told Gwen. "You run along too, darling. You know he would be hurt if you didn't visit."

"Oh, well, I...." Seeing the amusement on Luke's face, Gwen continued smoothly, "I'll visit him, Mama, another time. I told Tillie I'd help her do some canning."

"Nonsense." Anabelle flitted to the screen door, beaming at Luke as he held it open for her. "Thank you, darling," she said before giving Gwen a look over her shoulder. "You're on vacation. That's no time to be standing in a hot kitchen over boiling tomatoes. Run along and have fun. She's always loved to fish," she added to Luke before she stepped inside. "Tell Malon I'd adore some fresh shrimp." The door closed behind her. Gwen had the odd feeling that she had just been pushed gently out of the way. Luke gave her slim blue jeans and plain white T-shirt a cursory glance.

"Looks like you're dressed for fishing," he said with a nod. "Let's go."

"I have no intention of going anywhere with you." Gwen dusted her hands on her hips and started to move by him. She was brought up short by his hand on her arm. They stood side by side. Gwen let her eyes rest on his imprisoning hand and then slid them slowly to meet his. It was her most disdainful stare. "I beg your pardon?" she said icily. To her dismay, Luke burst out laughing. The warm, deep tones of it caused a bird to dart from the lawn to the shelter of a tree. "Let me go, you—you—"

"Wasn't it 'beast' before?" he asked as he began to assist her down the stairs.

"You are the most outrageous man." She continued to struggle as she trotted to keep pace.

"Thanks."

Gwen dug in her heels and managed to persuade Luke to stop. Staring up at him, she took a long, deep breath. "You are the most arrogant, officious, egotistical, thick-skinned man I have ever met."

"You forgot unreasonable, tyrannical and incredibly attractive. Really, Gwen, you surprise me. I thought you had more imagination. Are those your best insults?"

"Off the cuff, yes." She sniffed and tried not to respond to the humor in his eyes. "If you'll give me a little time, I can be more articulate."

"Don't trouble, I got the idea." He released her arm, held up one hand in the air, and the other out to her. "Truce?"

Gwen's guard relaxed before she realized it. Her hand moved to meet his.

"Truce," she agreed with only a token trace of reluctance.

"Until...?" he asked as he rubbed his thumb lightly across the back of her hand.

"Until I decide to be annoyed with you again." Gwen smiled, tossing back her curls as she enjoyed his laugh. It was, she decided, the most pleasing, infectious laugh she had ever heard.

"Well, will you fish with me?" he asked.

"Perhaps I will." For a moment she pursed her lips in thought. When she smiled again, it was the smile of challenge. "Ten bucks says I catch a bigger fish than you."

"Done." Casually, Luke laced his fingers through hers. This time Gwen made no objection.

Gwen knew every twist of the river and every turn of the paths in the bayou. Automatically, she moved north toward Malon's cabin. They walked under cascading moss and filtered sunlight.

"Do you really know how to can tomatoes, Gwenivere?" Luke asked as he bent under a low-hanging branch.

"Certainly, and anything else that comes out of a garden. When you're poor, a garden can mean the difference between eating or not."

"I've never known poor people who eat with Georgian silver," Luke commented dryly.

"Heirlooms." Gwen gave a sigh and a shrug. "Mama always considered heirlooms a sacred trust. One can't sell a sacred trust. Nor," she added with a wry smile, "can one comfortably wear or eat a sacred trust. Mama loves that house, it's her Camelot. She's a woman who needs a Camelot."

"And Gwenivere doesn't?" A great egret, startled by their intrusion, unfolded himself from the water and rose into the sky. Gwen felt an old, familiar stir of pleasure as she watched.

"I suppose I've always wanted to find my own. Heirlooms belong to someone else first. I'd nearly forgotten the scent of wild jasmine," she murmured as the fragrance drifted to her.

There was a dreamlike stillness around them. Beside them, the stream moved on its lackadaisical journey to the Gulf. Its water mirrored the moss-dripping trees. Gwen tossed a pebble and watched the ripples spread and vanish. "I spent most of my leisure time out here when I was younger," she said. "I felt more at home here than inside my own house. There was never any real privacy there with strangers always coming and going. I never wanted to share my kingdom with anyone before...."

She could feel Luke's big hand tighten his grasp on hers. He met her eyes with perfect understanding.

Chapter Nine

Malon's cabin hung over the water. It was built of split logs with a low, wide A roof and a porch that doubled as a dock for his *pirogue*. On a small, spare patch of grass beside the cabin, half a dozen chickens clucked and waddled. Somewhere deep in the marsh, a woodpecker drummed. A scratchy recording of music by Saint-Saëns came from the cabin to compete with the drumming and clucking. Stretched lengthwise on a narrow railing above the water, a tabby cat slept.

"It's just the same," Gwen murmured. She was unaware of the relief in her voice or the pleasure that lit her face. She smiled up at Luke and pulled him quickly across the lawn and up the three wooden steps. "Raphael," she said to the snoozing cat. Lazily he opened one eye, made a disinterested noise and shut it again. "Affectionate as ever," Gwen remarked. "I was afraid he'd forget me."

"Raphael is too old to forget anything."

Gwen turned quickly at the sound of the voice. Malon stood in the cabin doorway, a mortar and pestle in his hand. He was a small man, barely taller than Gwen herself, but with powerful arms and shoulders. His middle had not gone to flesh with age, but remained as flat as a boxer's, as he had indeed once been. His hair was white, thick and curly, his face brown and lined, his eyes a faded blue under dark brows. His age was a mystery. The bayou had been his home for an unspecified number of years. He took from the stream what he needed and was content. He had both a passionate love and a deep respect for the bayou. These he had passed on to the young girl who had found his cabin more than fifteen years before. Gwen checked the impulse to run into his arms.

"Hello, Malon. How are you?"

"Comme ci, comme ça." He gave a tiny shrug, then set down his mortar and pestle. He nodded a greeting to Luke before concentrating on Gwen. For a full minute she stood silent under his scrutiny. At length he said, "Let me see your hands." Obediently, Gwen held them out. "Soft," Malon said with a

snort. "Lady's hands now, *hein?* Why didn't you get a lady's figure in New York too?"

"I could only afford the hands. I'm still saving up for the rest. And Tillie's still pressing your shirts, I see," Gwen ran an experimental finger over the faded but crisp material of his cotton shirt. "When are you going to marry her?"

"I'm too young to get married," he said. "I have not finished sowing wild oats."

Gwen laughed and laid her cheek against his. "Oh, I've missed you, Malon." He answered her laugh and gave her one quick, bruising and unexpected hug. From the outset, they had spoken in Cajun French, a dialect that Gwen used again without the slightest thought. She closed her eyes a moment, enjoying the strength in his burly arms, the feel of his leathery cheek against hers, the scent of woodsmoke and herbs that was his personal cologne. She realized suddenly why she had not come to see him earlier. He had been the one constant male figure in her life. She had been afraid she would find him changed.

"Everything's the same," she murmured.

"But you." There was a smile in his voice, and she heard it.

"I should have come sooner." For the first time since she had known him, Gwen dared kiss his cheek.

"You are forgiven," he said.

Gwen was suddenly conscious of Luke beside her. She flushed. "I'm sorry," she said to him, "I—I didn't realize that we were rambling on in French."

Luke smiled while absently scratching Raphael's ears. "You don't have to apologize—I enjoyed it."

Gwen forced her thoughts into order. She would not fall under the charm of that smile again. "Do you speak French?" she asked with casual interest.

"No. But I still enjoyed it." She had the uncomfortable feeling he knew precisely how deeply his smile affected her. He turned his clear, calm eyes to Malon. "Anabelle says she'd like some shrimp."

"I go shrimping tomorrow," Malon answered with an agreeable nod. "Your book goes well?"

"Well enough."

"So, you take the day off, *hein?* You take this one fishing?" A jerk of his thumb in Gwen's direction accompanied the question.

"Thought I might," Luke replied without glancing at her.

Malon shrugged and sniffed. "Use t'be she knew which end of the pole to hold and which to put in the water, but that was before she went up there." A snap of his head indicated "up there." Even a town twenty miles from Lafitte was regarded with suspicion.

"Perhaps she remembers," Luke suggested. "She seems reasonably intelligent."

"She was raised good," Malon added, softening a bit. "Her papa was a good boy. She has his face. She don't favor her mama."

Gwen straightened her shoulders and raised her brows ever so slightly. "*She* remembers *everything*. My mother can outfish both of you in her sleep."

"Poo-yie!" Malon shook his hand and wrist as if he had touched something hot. "This city girl, she scare me out of my shoe. You take her. Me, I'm too old to fight with mean women."

"A minute ago you were too young to get married," Gwen reminded him.

"Yes, it's a good age I have." He smiled contentedly. "*Allez,* I have medicine to make. Take the poles and the *pirogue* and bring me a fish for my dinner." Without another word, he walked into the cabin, letting the screen door slam shut behind him.

"He hasn't changed," Gwen stated, trying to sound indignant.

"No," Luke agreed, taking two fishing poles and putting them across his shoulder. "He's still crazy about you." After stepping into the *pirogue*, he held out a hand to her. With the ease of experience, Gwen settled into the canoe. Soundlessly, Raphael leaped from rail to boat and fell instantly back to sleep.

"He doesn't want to miss the fun," Gwen explained.

Luke poled away from the dock. "Tell me, Gwenivere," he asked, "how do you come to speak the dialect so fluently? Anabelle can barely read a French menu." Sunshine dappled their heads as they passed under a canopy of trees.

"Tillie taught me." Gwen leaned her head back and let the warm sunlight play on her face. She remembered Malon saying long ago that his *pirogue* could ride on a film of dew. "I've spoken the coastal dialect for as long as I can remember. For the most part, the people here treat outsiders as beneath their notice; it's a very closed society. But I speak Cajun—therefore, I *am* Cajun. I'm curious, though, why Malon accepts you. It's obvious that you're on easy terms."

"I don't speak Cajun." Luke stood in the *pirogue* and poled down the river as if born to it. "But we speak the same language nonetheless."

They cleared the trees and drifted into a ghost forest shadowed by stumps of cypress. The boat moved through floating mats of hyacinths. Tiny baby crawfish clung to the clumped roots, while a fat cottonmouth disappeared into the lavender blooms. The winding river was teeming with life. Gwen watched a marsh raccoon fishing from the sloping bank.

"How is it," Gwen mused aloud, "that a Pulitzer Prize winner speaks the same language as a Louisiana *traiteur*?"

"*Traiteur?*" Luke repeated, meeting the frank curiosity in her eyes.

"Folk doctor. Malon fishes and trades and lumbers sometimes, but primarily he's the local *traiteur*. He cures snakebites, illness and spells. Spells are his specialty."

"Hmm. Did you ever wonder why he lives here, alone with his cat, his music and his books?" Gwen did not answer, content to watch Luke pole through the scattered stumps. "He's been to Rome and London and Budapest, but he lives here. He's driven tanks, broken horses, boxed and flown planes. Now he fishes and cures spells. He knows how to fix a carburetor, how to play classical guitar and how to cure snakebites. He does as he pleases and no more. He's the most successful man I know."

"How did you find out so much about him in such a short time?"

"I asked," Luke told her simply.

"No. No, it's not as easy as that." Gwen made a frustrated gesture with her hand. "People tell you things, I don't know why. I've told you things I have no business telling you, and I tell you before I realize it." She examined his face. "And worse, you don't always need to be told, you know. You see people much too clearly."

He smiled down at her. "Does it make you uncomfortable that I know who you are?"

The river widened. Gwen's pout became a frown. "Yes, I think it does. It makes me feel defenseless, the same way I felt when I first saw Bradley's sketches.''

"An invasion of privacy?"

"Privacy's important to me," Gwen admitted.

"I understand," Luke leaned on the pole. "You grew up having to share your home with strangers, having to share Anabelle. The result is a desire for privacy and independence. I apologize for invading your privacy, but, after all, it's partly my profession."

"Are we all characters to you?" Gwen asked as she baited her hook and cast her line.

"Some more than others," he returned dryly, casting his line on the opposite side of the boat from hers.

Gwen shook her head. "You know," she began, then settled back, stretching her legs and crossing them, "I'm finding it very hard not to like you."

At the other end of the canoe, Luke mirrored her position. "I'm a very charming person."

"Unfortunately, that's true." With a contented sigh, Gwen closed her eyes. "You're not at all how I pictured you."

"Oh?"

"You look more like a woodchopper than a world-renowned writer."

Luke grinned. "And how should a world-renowned writer look?"

"Several different ways, I suppose. Intellectual, with small glasses and narrow shoulders. Or prominent..."

"Heaven forbid."

"Or prominent," Gwen continued, ignoring him. "Wearing a well-cut suit and with just a hint of a paunch. Dashing maybe, with a faint scar along the jawline. Or Byronic..."

"Oh, good Lord."

"With a romantic pallor and tragic eyes."

"It's difficult to maintain a pallor in California."

"The trouble is, you're too physical." Gwen was enjoying the gentle drift of the boat and the warm fingers of sun. "What's your new book about?"

"A man and a woman."

"It's been done before," Gwen commented as she opened her eyes.

Luke smiled. His legs made a friendly tangle with hers. "It's *all* been done before, child. It's simply that each person believes his is a fresh experience.''

Gwen tilted her head, waiting for his explanation.

Luke obliged. ''Endless numbers of symphonies are composed on the same eighty-eight keys.'' He closed his eyes, and Gwen took the opportunity to study him.

''Will you let me read it?'' she asked suddenly. ''Or are you temperamental and sensitive?''

''I'm only temperamental when it's to my advantage,'' Luke told her lazily, opening one eye. ''How's your spelling?''

''Comme ci, comme ça,'' Gwen grinned across at him.

''You can proof my rough draft, my spelling's only half that good.''

''That's generous of you.'' Abruptly she let out a cry. ''Oh, I've got one!'' Instantly she was sitting up, giving all her attention to the fish on the end of her line. Her face was animated as she tossed her hair back with an impatient jerk of her head. There was competence in her hands and a gleam of challenge in her eyes. ''Eight pounds easy,'' she announced as she plopped the defeated fish on deck. "And that was just for practice." Raphael roused himself to inspect the first catch, then curled up beside Gwen's hip and went back to sleep.

The silence lay comfortably between them. There was no need for conversation or small talk. Dragonflies streaked by now and then with a flash of color and a quick buzz. Occasionally birds called to each other. It seemed natural to Gwen to loll drowsily across from Luke under the hazy sun. Her legs crossed over his with absent camaraderie. The shadows lengthened. Still they lingered, drifting among the stumps of once-towering cypress.

"The sun'll be gone in a couple of hours," Luke commented. Gwen made an unintelligible sound of agreement. "We should be heading back." The boat rocked gently as Luke got to his feet.

Under the cover of gold-tipped lashes, Gwen watched him. He stretched and muscles rippled. His eyes were clear and light, an arresting contrast to the burnished tone of his skin. They flicked over her as she lay still, too comfortable to stir herself. She knew that he was aware of her scrutiny.

"You owe me ten dollars," she reminded him smiling.

"A small price to pay for the afternoon." The water sighed as the boat glided over it. "Did you know you have five pale gold freckles on your nose?"

Gwen laughed as she stretched her arms luxuriously over her head. "I believe you're quite mad."

He watched her as the lashes shadowed her cheeks and her mouth sweetened with a smile. "I begin to be sure of it," he murmured.

It wasn't until the *pirogue* bumped noiselessly against its home dock that Gwen stirred again. The thin wisps of clouds were pink now with the setting sun, and there was a coolness in the air.

"Mmm." Her sigh was filled with the simple pleasure of the moment. "What a lovely ride."

"Next time, you pole," Luke stated. He watched Raphael stand, stretch and leap nimbly onto the dock and then joined him. After securing the boat, he offered a hand to Gwen.

"I suppose that's only fair." Gwen stood in one fluid movement. As nimbly as Raphael, she leaped onto the dock. She tilted back her head to give Luke a flippant grin, but found her lips captured by his.

One hand tangled in her hair while his other pressed into the small of her back, demanding she come closer. His mouth was desperate in its need for possession. There was a tension in him, a whisper of power held tightly in check. Gwen's pulses hammered at the thought of it unleashed. There was no gentleness in the mouth that claimed hers nor in the arms that held her, and she asked for none. There was a wild, restless thing in her that cried for release. She explored the strength of his arms, then the softness of his hair as she plunged deeper into sensations she could no longer measure. Touching him, she felt there were no limits to the power flooding her. What filled her was more than the quick heat of passion, more than a transient surge of desire. It was an all-consuming need to be his. She wanted to travel where only he could take her and to learn what only he could teach her. Then Luke's hands were on her shoulders, pushing her away.

"Gwen," he began in a voice roughened with desire.

"No, don't talk," she murmured and pulled his mouth back to hers. It was his taste, and his taste only, that could satisfy her growing hunger. She was famished, only now aware that she had fasted all her life. For a soaring, blinding moment, his mouth bruised hers; then he wrenched away. He held her shoulders in a crushing grip, but Gwen felt no pain as his eyes met hers. She could only stare. Her confusion, her need, her willingness were plain on her face. Luke's oath was savage and swift as he turned away.

"You should know better than to look at a man like that."

Gwen heard the harsh journey of air in and out of his lungs. Her fingers shook as she ran them nervously through her hair. "I—I don't know how I looked."

"Malleable," Luke muttered. He stared down at the sluggish river before turning back to her. "Pliant, willing and outrageously innocent. Do you know how difficult it is to resist the untouched, the uncorrupted?"

Helplessly, Gwen shook her head. "No, I...."

"Of course you don't," Luke cut in sharply. She winced at his tone, and he let out a long breath. "Good Heavens, how easy it is to forget what a child you are."

"I'm not, I..." Gwen shook her head in mute denial. "It happened so fast, I didn't think. I just...."

"I can hardly deny that it's my fault." His tone had cooled, and its marked disinterest had the edge of a knife. "You're an extraordinary creature, part will-o'-the-wisp, part Amazon, and I have a problem keeping my hands off you. Knowing I can have you is not exactly an incentive to restrain myself."

His matter-of-fact tone scraped at Gwen's raw pride even as it tripped her temper. "You're hateful."

"Agreed," Luke said with a brief nod. "But still, I think, civilized enough not to take advantage of an innocent girl."

"I am not...." Gwen managed before she felt the need to swallow. "I am not an innocent girl, I'm a grown woman!"

"As you wish. Do you still want me to take advantage of you?" Luke's tone was agreeable now.

"No!" Impatiently, she brushed at the hair on her forehead. "I mean, it wouldn't be.... Certainly not!"

"In that case...." Taking her arm, Luke firmly guided Gwen inside Malon's cabin.

Chapter Ten

Knocking on Luke's door was not the easiest thing Gwen had ever done, but it was necessary. She felt it necessary to prove to herself that she would not succumb to a newly discovered weakness again. She was a grown woman, capable of handling herself. She had asked to read Luke's manuscript, had agreed to proof it. She would not back down because of a kiss or a moment of madness. Still, Gwen braced herself as she lifted her knuckles to the wood. She held her breath.

"Come in."

These simple, ordinary words from inside the room caught at her heart. Letting out her breath slowly, she arranged her features in casual, almost indifferent lines and opened the door. Luke did not even bother to look up.

Reference books were piled on the table and scattered over the floor. Papers—typewritten, handwritten, crumpled and smooth—

were strewn everywhere. On the table in the midst of the chaos was a battered portable typewriter. There sat the creator of the havoc, frowning at the keys while he pounded on them. The curtains were still drawn, closing out the late morning sun, and the bed was a tangle of sheets. Everywhere were books, papers, folders.

"What a mess," Gwen murmured involuntarily. At her voice, Luke glanced up. There was at first a crease of annoyance between his brows, then a look of mild surprise before all was smoothed away.

"Hello," he said easily. He did not rise, but leaned back in his chair to look at her.

Gwen advanced, stepping over books and around papers on the journey. "This is incredible." She lifted her hand to gesture around the room, then dropped it to her side. "How do you live like this?"

Luke looked around, shrugged and met the curiosity in her eyes. "I don't, I work like this. If you've come to tidy up, I'll tell you the same thing I told the girl Anabelle used to send up here. Mess with my papers, and I'll toss you out the window."

Amused, Gwen stuck her hands in her pockets and nudged a book out of her way with her toe. "So, you're temperamental after all." This, she felt, was a trait she could understand and deal with.

"If you like," he agreed. "This way, if I lose something, I can only swear at myself, not at some hapless maid or well-meaning secretary. I have an aversion for well-meaning secretaries. What can I do for you? I'm afraid the coffee's cold."

The formality in his tone made it clear this was his domain. Gwen schooled her voice to sound briskly professional. "You said yesterday you'd like me to proof your manuscript. I'd be glad to do it, if," she added with a glance around the room, "you can find it."

He smiled his charming, irresistible smile. Gwen hardened herself against it. "Are you an organized soul, Gwenivere? I've always admired organization as long as it doesn't infringe on my habits. Sit," he invited with a gesture of his hand.

Gwen stepped over two dictionaries and an encyclopedia. "Would you mind if I opened the drapes first?" she asked.

"If you wish," he answered as he reached for a pile of typewritten pages. "Just don't get domestic."

"Nothing could be further from my mind," she assured him and had the pleasure of seeing him wince at the brilliance of the sunlight that streamed into the room. "There," she said, adopting the tone of a nursery school teacher, "isn't that better?"

"Sit."

Gwen did so after removing a pile of magazines from the chair across from him.

"You look older with your hair up," Luke commented mildly. "Nearly sixteen."

A fire lit in her eyes, but she managed to keep her voice cool. "Do you mind if I get started?"

"Not at all." Luke handed her a stack of typewritten material. "You'll find a pencil and a dictionary somewhere. Do as much as you like, just be quiet about it."

Gwen's mouth opened to retort, but as he was typing again, she closed it. After locating a pencil under a pile of discarded magazines, she picked up the first page. She refused to admit that the project excited her, that she wanted the job because it meant sharing something with him. Dismissing such thoughts, she determined to read with objective professionalism. Minutes later her pencil was forgotten—she was enthralled.

Time passed. Gwen no longer heard the clicking of the typewriter. Dust motes danced in the insistent sunlight, but Gwen was unaware of them. Luke's characters were flesh and blood to her. She felt she knew them, cared about them. She was even unaware that her eyes had filled with tears. She felt as the woman in Luke's story felt; desperately in love, confused, proud, vulnerable. She wept for the beauty of the words and the despair of the heroine. Suddenly, she lifted her eyes.

Luke had stopped typing, but for how long, she did not know. She blinked to clear her vision. He was watching her. His eyes were intent and searching, his mouth unsmiling. Helplessly Gwen stared back, letting the tears fall freely. Her weakness frightened her. He was not touching her, not speaking to her, yet her whole body felt attuned to him. She opened her mouth, but no words came. She shook her head, but he neither moved nor spoke. Knowing her only defense was escape, Gwen stood and darted from the room.

The bayou offered a haven, so she abandoned the house and fled toward it. She had calmed herself considerably by the time she neared Malon's cabin. Taking long, deep breaths, Gwen slowed her steps. It would not do to have Malon see her out of breath and distressed. As she rounded the last bend in the path, she saw Malon stepping from his *pirogue* onto the dock. Already, she felt reason returning.

"A good catch?" she asked, grateful she could smile at him without effort.

"Not bad," he answered with typical understatement. "Did you come for dinner?"

"Dinner?" Gwen repeated, glancing automatically at the sun. "Is it so late?" Could the afternoon have gone so swiftly? she wondered.

"It is late enough because I'm hungry," Malon replied. "We'll cook up some shrimp and eat, then you can take your mama her share. Can you still make coffee?"

"Of course I can still make coffee—just don't tell Tillie." Gwen followed him inside, letting the screen door slam behind them.

Before long the cabin was filled with the pungent scent of shrimp gumbo cooking and the quiet strains of Chopin. Raphael sunned on the windowsill, leaving the humans to deal with the domestic chores. Gwen felt the tension draining from her system. She ate, surprised at her appetite until she recalled she had eaten nothing since breakfast.

"You still like my cooking, *hein?*" Pleased, Malon spooned more gumbo onto her plate.

"I just didn't want to hurt your feelings," Gwen told him between bites. Malon watched her clean her plate and chuckled. With a contented sigh, Gwen sat back. "I haven't eaten that much in two years."

"That's why you're skinny." Malon leaned back, too, and lit a strong French cigarette. Gwen remembered the scent as well as she remembered the tastes. She had been twelve—curious and ultimately sick—when she had persuaded Malon to let her try one. He had offered no sympathy and no lecture. Grinning at the memory, Gwen watched the thin column of smoke rise.

"Now you feel better," Malon commented. At his statement, she shifted her eyes back to his. Instantly, she saw he was not referring to her hunger. Her shoulders lifted and then fell with her sigh.

"Some. I needed to come here—it's helped. I'm having trouble understanding myself, and there's . . . well, there's this man."

"There is bound to be," Malon agreed, blowing a series of smoke rings. "You are a woman."

"Yes, but not a very smart one. I don't know very much about men. And he's nothing like the men I've known in any case." She turned to Malon. "The trouble is. . . ." She made a small, frustrated sound and walked to the window. "The trouble is, I'm becoming more involved, more emotionally involved with . . . this man than I can afford to."

" 'Afford to,' " he repeated with a snort. "What do you mean, 'afford to'? Emotions cost you nothing."

"Oh, Malon." When she turned back to him, her eyes were unhappy. "Sometimes they cost everything. I'm beginning to need him, beginning to feel an—an attachment that can lead nowhere."

"And why can it lead nowhere?"

"Because I need love." After running a hand through her hair, Gwen paced the width of the cabin.

"So does everyone," Malon told her, carefully crushing out his cigarette.

"But he doesn't love me," she said miserably. Her hands made a futile gesture. "He doesn't love me, yet I can't stop thinking about him. When I'm with him I forget everything else. It's wrong, he's involved with someone else, and.... Oh, Malon, it's so complicated." Her voice faltered away.

"Life is not simple, little girl," he said, reverting to her childhood title, "but we live it." Rising, he moved toward her, then patted her cheek. "Complications provide spice."

"Right now," she said with a small smile, "I'd rather be bland."

"Did you come for advice or for sympathy?" His eyes were small and sharp, his palm rough. He smelled of fish and tobacco. Gwen felt the ground was more solid where he stood.

"I came to be with you," she told him softly, "because you are the only father I have." Slipping her arms around his waist, she rested her head on one of his powerful shoulders. She felt his wide hand stroke her hair. "Malon," she murmured. "I don't want to be in love with him."

"So, do you come for an antilove potion? Do you want a snake skin for his pillow?"

Gwen laughed and tilted back her head. "No."

"Good. I like him. I would feel bad putting a hex on him."

She realized Malon had known all along she had been speaking of Luke. Always she had been as clear as a piece of glass to him. Still, she was more comfortable with him than with anyone else. Gwen studied him, wondering what secrets he held behind the small blue eyes. "Malon, you never told me you'd been to Budapest."

"You never asked."

She smiled and relaxed. "If I asked now, would you tell me?"

"I'll tell you while you do the dishes."

Bradley frowned at his canvas, then at his model. "You're not giving me the spark," he complained as he pushed the fisherman's cap further back on his head.

Three nights of fitful sleep had dimmed Gwen's spark considerably. She sat, as Bradley had directed her, in the smoothly worn U formed by two branches of an ancient oak. She wore the robe he had chosen with a magnolia tucked behind her ear. Following his instructions, she had left her hair free and kept her makeup light. Because of their size and color, her eyes dominated the picture. But they did not, as Bradley had anticipated, hold the light he had seen before. There was a listlessness in the set of her shoulders, a moodiness in the set of her mouth.

"Gwen," Bradley said with exaggerated patience, "depression is not the mood we're seeking."

"I'm sorry, Bradley." Gwen shrugged and sent him a weary smile. "I haven't been sleeping well."

"Warm milk," Monica Wilkins stated from her perch on a three-legged stool. She was painting, with quiet diligence, a tidy clump of asters. "Always helps me."

Gwen wanted to wrinkle her nose at the thought, but instead she answered politely. "Maybe I'll try that next time."

"Don't scald it though," Monica warned as she perfected her image of a petal.

"No, I won't," Gwen assured her with equal gravity.

"Now that we've got that settled...." Bradley began in such a martyr-like voice that Gwen laughed.

"I'm sorry, Bradley, I'm afraid I'm a terrible model."

"Nonsense," Bradley said. "You've just got to relax."

"Wine," Monica announced, still peering critically at her asters.

"I beg your pardon?" Bradley turned his head and frowned.

"Wine," Monica repeated. "A nice glass of wine would relax her beautifully."

"Yes, I suppose it might if we had any." Bradley adjusted the brim of his cap and studied the tip of his brush.

"I have," Monica told him in her wispy voice.

"Have what?"

Gwen's eyes went back to Bradley. I'm beginning to feel as though I was at a tennis match, she thought, lifting a hand to the base of her neck.

"Wine," Monica answered, carefully adding a vein to a pale green leaf. "I have a thermos of white wine in my bag. It's nicely chilled."

"How clever of you," Bradley told her admiringly.

"Thank you." Monica blushed. "You're certainly welcome to it if you think it might help." Carefully she opened a bulky macrame sack and pulled out a red thermos.

"Monica, I'm in your debt." Gallantly, Bradley bowed over the thermos. Monica let out what sounded suspiciously like a giggle before she went back to her asters.

"Bradley, I really don't think this is necessary," Gwen began.

"Just the thing to put you into the mood," he disagreed as he unscrewed the thermos lid. Wine poured light and golden into the plastic cup.

"But Bradley, I hardly drink at all."

"Glad to hear it." He held out the cup. "Bad for your health."

"Bradley," Gwen began again, trying to keep her voice firm. "It's barely ten o'clock in the morning."

"Yes, drink up, the light will be wrong soon."

"Oh, good grief." Defeated, Gwen lifted the plastic cup to her lips and sipped. With a sigh, she sipped again. "This is crazy," she muttered into the wine.

"What's that, Gwen?" Monica called out.

"I said this is lovely," Gwen amended. "Thank you, Monica."

"Glad to help." As the women exchanged smiles, Bradley tipped more wine into the cup.

"Drink it up," he ordered like a parent urging medicine on a child. "We don't want to lose the light."

Obediently, Gwen tilted the cup. When she handed it back to Bradley, she heaved a huge sigh. "Am I relaxed?" she asked. There was a pleasant lightness near the top of her head. "My, it's gotten warm, hasn't it?" She smiled at no one in particular as Bradley replaced the lid on the thermos.

"I hope I haven't overdone it," he muttered to Monica.

"One never knows about people's metabolisms," Monica said. With a noncommittal grunt, Bradley returned to his canvas.

"Now look this way, love," he ordered as Gwen's attention wandered. "Remember, I want contrasts. I see the delicacy of your bone structure, the femininity in the pose, but I want to see character in your face. I want spirit—no, more—I want challenge in your eyes. Dare the onlooker to touch the untouched."

"Untouched," Gwen murmured as her memory stirred. "I'm not a child," she asserted and straightened her shoulders.

"No," Bradley agreed as he studied her closely. "Yes, yes, that's perfect!" He grabbed his brush. Glancing over his shoulder he caught sight of Luke approaching and then he gave his full attention to his work. "Ah, the mouth's perfect," he muttered, "just between sulky and a pout. Don't change it, don't change a thing. Bless you, Monica!"

Bradley worked feverishly, unaware that the wine was a far less potent stimulant to his model than the man who now stood beside him. It was his presence that brought the rush of color to her cheeks, that brightened her eyes with challenge and made her mouth grow soft, sulky and inviting. Luke's own face was inscrutable as he watched. Though he stood in quiet observation, there was an air of alertness about him. Bradley muttered as he worked. A crow cawed monotonously in the distance.

A myriad of thoughts and feelings rushed through Gwen's mind. Longing warred fiercely with pride. Luke had infuriated her, charmed her, laughed at her, rejected her. I will not fall in love with him, she told herself. I will not allow it to happen. *He won't make a fool of me again.*

"Magnificent," Bradley murmured.

"Yes, it is." Luke slipped his hands into his pockets as he studied the portrait. "You've caught her."

"It's rare," Bradley muttered, touching up the shadows of Gwen's cheeks in the portrait. "Her looks are just a bonus. It's that aura of innocence mixed with the hint of banked fires. Incredible combination. Every man who sees this portrait will want her."

A flash of irritation crossed Luke's face as he lifted his eyes to Gwen's. "Yes, I imagine so."

"I'm calling it *The Virgin Temptress*. It suits, don't you think?"

"Hmm."

Taking this as full agreement, Bradley lapsed back into unintelligible mutters. Abruptly, he put down his brush and began packing his equipment. "You did beautifully," he told Gwen. "We're losing the morning light. We should start a bit earlier, I think. Three more good sittings should do it now."

"I'll walk back with you, Bradley." Monica rose. "I've done about all I can do on this one." Gathering up her paints, easel and stool, she started after Bradley.

Gwen slipped down from her seat in the fork of the tree with a quick flutter of white. As her bare feet touched the grass, the wine spun dizzily in her head. Instinctively she rested her hand against the tree for support. Watching her, Luke lifted a brow in speculation. With exaggerated care, she straightened, swallowed the odd dryness in her throat and started to walk. Her legs felt strangely weak. It was her intention to walk past Luke with icy dignity, but he stopped her easily with a hand on her arm.

"Are you all right?"

The sun had the wine bubbling inside her. Clearing her throat, Gwen spoke distinctly. "Of course. I am just fine."

Luke placed two fingers under her chin and lifted it. He studied her upturned face. Humor leaped into his eyes. "Why, Gwenivere, you're sloshed."

Knowing the truth of his statement only stiffened her dignity. "I have no idea what you are talking about. If you would kindly remove your hand from my face, I would greatly appreciate it."

"Sure. But don't blame me if you fall on it once the support's gone." Luke dropped his hand, and Gwen swayed dangerously. She gripped Luke's shirt to right herself.

"If you will excuse me," she said regally, but neither moved nor dropped her hand. Heaving a deep sigh, Gwen raised her face again and frowned. "I'm waiting for you to stand still."

"Oh. Sorry. May one ask how you came to be in this condition?"

"Relaxed," Gwen corrected.

"I beg your pardon?"

"That's what I am. It was either wine or warm milk. Monica's a whiz at these things. I'm not too fond of warm milk, and there wasn't any handy in any case."

"No, I can see it might be difficult to come by," Luke agreed, slipping a supporting arm around her waist as she began to weave her way across the lawn.

"I only had a topful, you know."

"That should do it."

"Oh dear." Gwen stopped abruptly. "I've stepped on a bee." She sat down in a floating film of white. "I suppose the poor little thing will go off and die." Lifting her foot, she frowned at the small welt on the ball of her foot.

"Happily bombed, I should think." Luke sat down and took her foot in his hand. "Hurt?" he asked as he drew out the stinger.

"No, I don't feel anything."

"Small wonder. I think it might be wise to tell Bradley you don't want to be quite so relaxed at ten in the morning."

"He's very serious about his art," Gwen said confidentially. "He believes I'll become immoral."

"A distinct possibility if you continue to relax before noon," Luke agreed dryly. "But I believe you mean 'immortal.'"

"Do you think so too?" Gwen lifted her face to the sun. "I really thought he and Monica were macadamias."

"What?"

"Nuts." Gwen lay back in the grass and shut her eyes. "I think it would be rather sweet if they fell in love, don't you?"

"Adorable."

"You're just cynical because you've been in love so many times."

"Have I?" He traced a finger over her ankle as he watched the sun highlight her hair. "Why do you say that?"

"Your books. You know how women think, how they feel. When I was reading yesterday, I hurt because it was too real, too personal." The robe shifted lightly with her sigh. "I imagine you've made love with dozens of women."

"Making love and being in love are entirely separate things."

Gwen opened her eyes. "Sometimes," she agreed. "For some people."

"You're a romantic," Luke told her with a shrug. "Only a romantic can wear floating white or toss flowers to the stars or believe a magician's illusions."

"How odd." Gwen's voice was genuinely puzzled as she closed her eyes again. "I've never thought of myself as a romantic. Is it wrong?"

"No." The word was quick and faintly annoyed. Luke rose and stared down at her. Her hair was spread out under her, glinting with golden lights. The robe crossed lightly over her breasts, making an inviting shadow. Swearing under his breath, he bent and scooped her into his arms.

"Mmm, you're very strong." Her head spun gently, so she rested it against his shoulder. "I noticed that the first day, when I watched you chop down the tree. Michael lifts weights."

"Good for Michael."

"No, actually, he strained his back." With a giggle, Gwen snuggled deeper into the curve of his shoulder. "Michael isn't very physical, you see. He plays bridge." Gwen lifted her face and smiled cheerfully. "I'm quite hopeless at bridge. Michael says my mind needs discipline."

"I simply must meet this Michael."

"He has fifty-seven ties, you know."

"Yes, I imagine he does."

"His shoes are always shined," Gwen added wistfully and traced Luke's jawline with her fingertip. "I really must try to be more tidy. He tells me continually that the image a person projects is important, but I tend to forget. Feeding pigeons in the park isn't good for a corporate image."

"What is?"

"Opera," she said instantly. "German opera particularly, but I fall asleep. I like to watch murder mysteries on the late night T.V."

"Philistine," Luke concluded as his mouth twitched into a smile.

"Exactly," Gwen agreed, feeling more cheerful than she had in weeks. "Your face is leaner than his, too, and he never forgets to shave."

"Good for Michael," Luke mumbled again as he mounted the porch steps.

"He never made me feel the way you do." At these words Luke stopped and stared down into Gwen's eyes. Cushioned by the wine, Gwen met his look with a gentle smile. "Why do you suppose that is?"

Luke's voice was edged with roughness. "Can you really be so utterly guileless?"

She considered the question, then shrugged. "I don't know; I suppose so. Do you want me to be?"

For a moment, Luke's arms tightened, shifting her closer against him. In immediate response, Gwen closed her eyes and offered her mouth. When his lips brushed over her brow, she sighed and cuddled closer. "Sometimes you're a very nice man," she murmured.

"Am I?" He frowned down at her. "Let's say sometimes I remember there are a few basic rules. At the moment, I'm finding my memory unfortunately clear."

"A very nice man," Gwen repeated and kissed a spot under his jaw. With a yawn, she settled comfortably against him. "But I won't fall in love with you."

Luke looked down at her quiet face with its aureole of soft curls. "A wise decision," he said softly and carried her into the house.

Chapter Eleven

It was dark when Gwen awoke. Disoriented, she stared at the dim shapes of furniture and the pale silver moonlight. It was a knock at the door that had awakened her, and it came again, soft and insistent. Brushing her hair from her face, she sat up. The room spun once, then settled. Gwen moaned quietly and swallowed before she rose to answer the knock. In the hallway the light was bright. She put her hand over her eyes to shield them.

"Oh, darling, I'm sorry to wake you." Anabelle gave a sympathetic sigh. "I know how these headaches are."

"Headaches?" Gwen repeated, gingerly uncovering her eyes.

"Yes, Luke told me all about it. Did you take some aspirin?"

"Aspirin?" Gwen searched her memory. Abruptly, color rushed to her cheeks. "Oh!"

Taking this as an affirmative response, Anabelle smiled. "Are you feeling better now?"

"I haven't got a headache," Gwen murmured.

"Oh, I'm so glad, because you have a phone call." Anabelle smiled more brightly. "It's from New York, so I really thought it best to wake you. It's that Michael of yours. He has a lovely voice."

"Michael," Gwen echoed softly. She sighed, wishing she could return to the comforting darkness of her room. She felt only weariness at the sound of his name. Glancing down, she saw she still wore the white robe. She could clearly remember her conversation with Luke and, more disturbing, the feel of his arms as he carried her.

"You really shouldn't keep him waiting, darling." Anabelle interrupted Gwen's thoughts with gentle prompting. "It's long distance."

"No, of course not." Gwen followed her mother to the foot of the stairs.

"I'll just run along and have Tillie warm up some dinner for you." Anabelle retreated tactfully, leaving Gwen staring down at the waiting receiver. She took a deep breath, blew it out and picked up the phone.

"Hello, Michael."

"Gwen—I was beginning to think I'd been left on hold." His voice was even, well pitched and annoyed.

"I'm sorry." The apology was automatic, and immediately, she swore at herself for giving it. *Why does he always intimidate me?* she demanded silently of herself. "I was busy," she added in a firmer voice. "I wasn't expecting to hear from you."

"I hope it's a pleasant surprise," he replied. From the tone of his voice, Gwen knew he had already concluded it was. "I've been busy myself," he went on without bothering to hear her answer. "Right up to my chin in a lawsuit against Delron Corporation. Tricky business. It's had me chained to my desk."

"I'm sorry to hear that, Michael," Gwen said. Glancing up, she saw Luke coming down the steps. *Oh, perfect,* she thought in despair. She feigned unconcern with a faint nod of greeting, but when he stopped and leaned against the newel post, she frowned. "Do you mind?" she hissed at Luke in a whisper.

"No, not a bit." He smiled but made no effort to move. "Say hello for me."

Her eyes narrowed into furious slits. "You're horrible, absolutely horrible."

"What?" came Michael's puzzled voice. "What did you say?"

"Oh, nothing," Gwen said sharply.

"For heaven's sake, Gwen, I'm simply trying to tell you about the Delron case. You needn't get testy."

"I am not testy. Why did you call, Michael?"

"To see when you'd be coming home, sweetheart. I miss you." He was using his quiet, persuasive tone, and Gwen sighed. Closing her eyes, she rested the receiver against her forehead a moment.

"Does he always make you feel guilty?" Luke asked conversationally. Gwen jerked up her chin and glared.

"Shut up," she ordered, furious that he could read her so accurately.

"What?" Michael's voice shouted through the receiver. Luke gave a quick laugh at the outraged voice. "We must have a bad connection," he concluded.

"Must have," Gwen muttered. Taking a deep breath, Gwen decided to clear the air once and for all. "Michael, I...."

"I thought I'd given you enough time to cool off," Michael said pleasantly.

"Cool off?"

"It was foolish of us to fight that way, sweetheart. Of course I know you didn't mean the things you said."

"I didn't?"

"You know you have a tendency to say rash things when you're in a temper," Michael reminded her in a patient, forgiving tone. "Of course," he went on, "I suppose I was partially to blame."

"You were?" Gwen struggled to keep her voice quiet and reasonable. "How could you be partially to blame for my temper?" Glancing up, she saw Luke still watching her.

"I'm afraid I rushed you. You simply weren't ready for a sudden proposal."

"Michael, we've been seeing each other for nearly a year," Gwen reminded him, pushing her fingers through her hair in irritation. The gesture caused the V of her bodice to widen enticingly.

"Of course, sweetheart," he said soothingly. "But I should have prepared you."

"*Prepared me?* I don't want to be prepared, Michael, do you understand? I want to be surprised. And if you call me sweetheart again in that patronizing voice, I'm going to scream."

"Now, now, Gwen, don't get upset. I'm more than willing to forgive and forget."

"Oh." Gwen swallowed her rage. "Oh, that's generous of you, Michael. I don't know what to say."

"Just say when you'll be back, sweetheart. We'll have a nice celebration dinner and set the date. Tiffany's has some lovely rings; you can take your pick."

"Michael," Gwen said, "please listen to me. Really listen this time. I'm not what you want.... I can't be what you want. If I tried, I'd shrivel up inside. Please, I do care about you, but don't ask me to be someone I'm not."

"I don't know what you're talking about, Gwen," he interrupted. "I'm not asking you—"

"Michael," Gwen cut him off. "I just can't go through all this again. I did mean the things I said, but I don't want to have to say them all again. I'm not good for you, Michael. Find someone who knows how to fix vodka martinis for twenty.''

"You're talking nonsense." It was his cool attorney's voice, and Gwen closed her eyes, knowing arguments were futile. "We'll straighten all this out when you get home."

"No, Michael," she said, knowing he wouldn't hear.

"Give me a call and I'll meet your plane. Goodbye, Gwen."

"Goodbye, Michael," she murmured even while she replaced the receiver. She felt a wave of sorrow and guilt. Lifting her eyes, she met Luke's. There was no amusement in them now, only understanding. She felt that amusement would have been easier to handle. "I'd appreciate it very much," she said quietly, "if you wouldn't say anything just now." She walked past him and up the stairs while he looked after her.

Gwen stood on her balcony under a moonlit sky. Moss-draped cypress trees appeared ghostly and tipped with silver. There was a bird singing in a sweet, clear voice, and she wondered if it was a nightingale. The time seemed right for nightingales. She sighed, remembering that Luke had called her a romantic. Perhaps he was right. But it was not the soft night or the song of a bird that kept her out of bed and on the balcony.

Of course you can't sleep, she berated herself silently. How can you expect to sleep at night when you slept all afternoon? Color rushed to her cheeks as she recalled the reason for her peaceful midday nap. I certainly managed to make a first-class fool of myself. Did he have to be there? Couldn't I have stumbled into the house without an audience? Why can I never be cool and dignified around him?

And then the call from Michael. Gwen lifted her hand to the base of her neck and tried to massage away the tension. Again she played over the telephone conversation in her mind, attempting to find some way she could have made her feelings clearer. It's all been said before, she reminded herself, but he doesn't listen. *He forgives me.* With a quiet laugh, Gwen pressed her fingers to her eyes. He forgives me but thinks nothing of the cruel things he said. He doesn't even love me. He loves the woman he'd like me to be.

As she watched, a star shivered and fell in a speeding arc of light. Gwen caught her breath at the fleeting flash from heaven. Abruptly her thoughts centered on Luke. With him she had felt a meteoric intensity, a brilliant heat. But she knew she could not hold him anymore than the night sky could hold the trailing shimmer of light. Feeling a sudden chill, Gwen slipped back into her room. The middle of the night's a bad time for thinking, she decided. I'd be much better off if I went downstairs and tried some of Monica's detestable warm milk.

Gwen moved quickly down the hall, not bothering to switch on a light. She knew her way, just as she knew which steps creaked and which boards moaned. An unexpected sound made her whirl around as she reached the head of the stairs.

"Mama!" Stunned, Gwen watched her mother creep down the third-floor staircase. Anabelle started at Gwen's voice, and her hand fluttered to her heart.

"Gwenivere, you scared the wits out of me!" Anabelle's soft bosom rose with her breath. Her hair was charmingly disordered around her face. The robe she wore was frilly, pink and feminine. "Whatever are you doing out here in the dark?"

"I couldn't sleep." Gwen moved closer and caught the familiar scent of lilac. "Mama...."

"Of course, you're probably starving." Anabelle gave a sympathetic cluck. "It doesn't do to miss meals, you know."

"Mama, what were you doing upstairs?"

"Upstairs?" Anabelle repeated, then glanced back over her shoulder. "Oh, why, I was just up with Luke." She smiled, not noticing Gwen's draining color.

"W—with Luke?"

"Yes." She made a token gesture of tidying her hair. "He's such a marvelous, generous man."

Gwen gently took her mother's hand. "Mama." She bit her lip to steady her voice and took a deep breath. "Are you certain this is what you want?"

"Is what what I want, darling?"

"This—this relationship with Luke," Gwen managed to get out, although the words hurt her throat.

"Oh, Gwen, I simply couldn't get along without Luke." She gave Gwen's icy hand a squeeze. "Goodness, you're cold. You'd best get back to bed, dear. Is there anything I can get for you?"

"No," Gwen answered quietly. "No, there's nothing." She gave Anabelle a quick, desperate hug. "Please, you go back to bed, I'll be fine."

"All right, dear." Anabelle kissed her brow in a way Gwen recognized from childhood. Satisfied that there was no fever, Anabelle patted her cheek. "Good night, Gwen."

"Good night, Mama," Gwen murmured, watching her disappear down the hall.

Gwen waited until the sound of the closing door had echoed into silence before she let out a shuddering breath. Face it, Gwen, you've been falling for your mother's man. For a moment, she merely stared down at her empty hands. Doing nothing wasn't enough, she reflected. I could have stopped it.... I didn't want to stop it. There's nothing to do now but get untangled while I still can. It's time to face things head on. Lifting her chin, she began to climb the stairs to the third floor.

Without giving herself a chance to think any further, she knocked at Luke's door.

"Yes?" The reply was curt and immediate.

Refusing to give in to the urge to turn and run, Gwen twisted the knob and pushed open Luke's door. He was, as he had been before, seated in the midst of his own disorder. He was hitting the keys of the typewriter in a quick, staccato rhythm, and his eyes were intent and concentrated. Faded, low-slung jeans were his only concession to modesty. The faintest hint of lilac drifted through the air. Moistening her lips, Gwen kept her eyes from the tousled sheets of the bed.

I am in love with him, she realized suddenly and simultaneously remembered it was impossible for her to be so. I'll have to find a way to fall out of love with him, she told herself, warding off a brief stab of misery. I'll have to start now. Keeping her head high, she closed the door behind her and leaned against it.

"Luke?"

"Hmm?" He glanced up absently, his fingers still working the keys. His expression altered as he focused on her. His hands lay still. "What are you doing here?" There was such sharp impatience in his voice that Gwen bit her lip.

"I'm sorry to interrupt your work. I need to talk to you."

"At this hour of the night?" His tone was politely incredulous. "Run along, Gwen, I'm busy."

Gwen swallowed her pride. "Luke, please. It's important."

"So's my sanity," he muttered without changing rhythm.

She ran a hand through her hair. *Sanity,* she thought desperately, *I must have lost mine the moment he put down that axe and walked toward me.* "You're making this very difficult."

"I?" he tossed back furiously. "I make it difficult? Do you know how you look at me? Do you know how many times I've found myself alone with you when you're half dressed?" Instinctively, Gwen reached for the low neckline of her robe. "Contrary to popular opinion," he continued as he rose and strode to a small table across the room, "I am a mortal man given to normal instincts." There was a decanter of brandy on the table, and he poured himself a hefty glass. "Damn it, I want you. Haven't I made that clear enough?"

His tone was rough. Gwen felt the tears burn in her throat. When she spoke her voice was thick with them. "I'm sorry, I didn't mean...." She broke off with a helpless shrug.

"For God's sake, don't cry," he said impatiently. "I'm in no mood to give you a few comforting kisses and send you along. If I touch you now, you won't leave here tonight." His eyes met hers. She swallowed even the thought of tears. "I'm not in a civilized mood, Gwen. I told you once that I know my limit. Well, I've reached it." He lifted the decanter and poured again.

Temptation fluttered along her skin. He wanted her, she could almost taste his desire. How easy it would be to take just one small step... to steal a night, a moment. The night would be full and rich. *But the morning would be empty.* Gwen's eyes dropped and she struggled with her own heart. When his passion was spent, she knew her love would starve. Love has found another fool, she thought resignedly. It's best to do this quickly.

"This isn't easy for me," Gwen told him quietly. Though she fought for calm, her eyes were tragic as they met his. "I need to talk to you about Mama."

Luke turned and walked to the French doors. Tossing them open, he stared out into the night. "What about her?"

"I was wrong to interfere." Gwen shut her eyes tight and struggled to strengthen her voice. "It was wrong of me to come here thinking I had any say in whom my mother becomes involved with."

Luke swore and whirled back to face her. She watched him struggle with temper. "You are an idiot. Anabelle is a beautiful woman—"

"Please," Gwen interrupted swiftly, "let me finish. I need to say this, and it's so difficult. I'd like to say it all at once." She still stood with her back to the door, poised for escape. Luke shrugged, dropped back into his chair and signaled for her to continue. "It isn't up to me to decide what's right for my mother, it's not my right to interfere. You're good for her, I can't deny it." Gwen's breath trembled before she could steady it. "And I can't deny I'm attracted to you, but it's nothing that can't be resolved by a bit of distance. I think—I think if you and I just stay out of each other's way for the rest of my visit, everything will work out."

"Oh, do you?" Luke gave a quick laugh as he set down his glass. "That's an amazing piece of logic." He rubbed the bridge of his nose between his thumb and forefinger. Gwen frowned at the action, finding it somehow out of character.

"I'm leaving next week," Gwen told him. "There's no need for me to stay, and I've left several things undone back in New York." Hurriedly, she turned to the door.

"Gwen." Luke's voice stopped her, but she could not bear to turn and face him again. "Don't waste yourself on Michael."

"I don't intend to," she answered in a choked voice. Blind with tears, she opened the door and plunged into the darkness.

Chapter Twelve

Gwen dressed with care. She stretched out the process, dawdling over the buttons of her pale lavender blouse. After another sleepless night, Gwen knew she could not survive even a few more days in the same house with Luke. She could not be sophisticated, mature or philosophical about love. She went to her closet and pulled out her suitcase.

When two women love the same man, she mused, one of them has to lose. If it were anyone else, I could fight her. She opened the first case. How does a daughter fight her own mother? Even if she wins, she loses. I haven't really lost, she reflected as she moved to her dresser and pulled open a drawer. You have to have something first to lose it. I never had Luke.

Gwen packed methodically, using the task as a diversion. She refused to speculate on what she would do when she returned to New York. While packing, she had no past and no future, only the present. She would have to face the shambles of her life soon enough.

"Gwen." Anabelle knocked quickly and stuck her head into the room. "I wonder if you've seen.... Oh!" She opened the door all the way when she saw Gwen's half-packed cases. "What's this?"

Gwen moistened her lips and strove for casualness. "I've got to get back to New York."

"Oh." There was disappointment in the single syllable. "But you just got here. Are you going back to Michael?"

"No, Mama, I'm not going back to Michael."

"I see." She paused a moment. "Is there some trouble at your office?"

The excuse was so perfect, agreement trembled on Gwen's tongue. Regretfully, the lie would not form on her lips. "No."

Anabelle tilted her head at her daughter's tone, then quietly closed the door at her back. "You know I don't like to pry, Gwen, and I know you're a very private person, but...." Anabelle sighed before she walked over to sit on Gwen's bed. "I really think you'd better tell me what this is all about."

"Oh, Mama." Gwen turned away and rested both palms on her dresser. "It's such an awful mess."

"It can't be as bad as all that." Anabelle folded her hands neatly in her lap. "Just tell me straight out, it's the best way."

Gwen took a breath and held it. "I'm in love with Luke," she said quickly, then expelled the breath in one swift whoosh.

"And..." Anabelle prompted.

Gwen's eyes flew to the mirror in search of her mother's. "Mama, I said I was in love with Luke."

"Yes, darling, I heard that part. I'm waiting for the part about the dreadful mess."

"Mama." Gingerly, Gwen turned around. Anabelle smiled patiently. "It's not just an infatuation or a crush, I'm really in love with him."

"Oh yes, well, that's nice."

"I don't think you understand." Gwen covered her face with her hands for a moment and then dropped them. "I even wanted him to—to make love with me."

Anabelle blushed a soft, gentle pink and brushed at her skirts. "Yes, well...I'm sure that's quite natural. I don't believe you and I ever had a talk about...ah, the birds and the bees."

"Oh good grief, Mama," Gwen said impatiently. "I don't need a lecture on sex. I know all about that."

"Oh?" Anabelle lifted her brows in maternal censure. "I see."

"No, I don't mean...." Gwen stopped in frustration. How did this conversation get away from me? she wondered. "Mama, please, this is hard enough. I came home to get rid of the man, and before I knew it, I was involved with him. I didn't plan it, I didn't want it. I'd never, never do anything to hurt you, and I was wrong because years don't mean a thing, and no one has the right to choose for anyone else. Now I have to go away because I love you both so terribly, don't you see?" Gwen ended on a note of despair and dropped down at Anabelle's feet.

Anabelle stared down at the tragic face thoughtfully. "Perhaps I will in a minute," she answered, furrowing her brow. "No, actually, I don't think I will. Why don't you try again? Start with the part about your coming here to get rid of Luke; I believe that's where I got confused."

Gwen sniffled and accepted Anabelle's lace hankie. "I wanted to make him go away because I thought it was wrong for you to have an affair with him. But it was none of my—"

"A what?" Anabelle interrupted. Her hand paused on its journey to smooth Gwen's curls. *"An affair?"* she repeated, blinking rapidly.

"An affair? Luke and I?" To Gwen's amazement, Anabelle tossed back her head and laughed. It was a young, gay sound. "How delightful! Darling, darling, how flattering. My, my." She smiled into space, her cheeks rosy with pleasure. "Such a handsome young man too. He must be—" She stopped and fluttered her lashes, "well, a year or two younger than I." She laughed again and clapped her hands together as Gwen looked on. Bending down, she kissed her daughter soundly. "Thank you, sweet, sweet child. I don't know when I've had a nicer present."

"Now *I* don't understand." Gwen wiped a lingering tear from her lashes. "Are you saying you and Luke aren't lovers?"

"Oh, my." Anabelle rolled her eyes. "How very blunt you are."

"Mama, please, I'll go mad in a moment." Briefly, Gwen pressed her fingers to her eyes. Rising, she began to pace the room. "You talked and talked about him in all your letters. You said he'd changed your life. You said he was the most wonderful man you'd ever met. You couldn't get along without him. And just last night you were coming out of his room in the middle of the night. And you've been acting strangely." Gwen whirled around and paced in the other direction. "You can't deny it. Locking your door and practically pushing me out of the house on the flimsiest of excuses."

"Oh, dear." Anabelle clucked her tongue and touched a hand to her hair. "I begin to see. I suppose it was silly of me to keep it a secret." Standing, Anabelle took a blouse from Gwen's suitcase, shook it out and walked to the closet. "Yes, it's obviously my fault. But then, I wanted to surprise you. Poor darling, no wonder you've been so unhappy and confused. I'm afraid I thought you were brooding over Michael, but it wasn't him at all, was it? Luke makes much better sense, I'm sure." Carefully, Anabelle hung up the blouse. "Now, when I think back on it, I can see how you might think so." She moved back to the suitcase while Gwen prayed for patience. "Luke and I aren't having an affair, though I do thank you for the kind thought, dear. We are, however, collaborating in a sense. Why don't you sit down?"

"I think," Gwen said, "I'm going to scream any minute."

"Always so impatient," Anabelle sighed. "Well, this is a bit embarrassing. I feel so foolish." She placed her hands on her cheeks as they grew warm. "Oh, I do hope you won't laugh at me I'm . . . I'm writing a book." The confession came out in a swift jumble of words.

"What?" Gwen exclaimed, touching her hand to her ear to check her hearing.

"I've always wanted to, but I never thought I could until Luke encouraged me." Excitement joined the embarrassment in Anabelle's voice. "I've always had such pretty stories in my head, but I never had the courage to write them down. Luke says," Anabelle lifted her chin and glowed proudly, "he says I have a natural talent."

"Talent?" Gwen echoed as she sank onto the bed.

"Isn't that lovely of him?" Anabelle enthused. She shook out one of Gwen's packed dresses and moved toward the closet. "He's given me so much help, so much time and encouragement! He doesn't even mind if I pop up to his room and try out an idea! Why, just last night he stopped his own work to listen to me."

Remembering the conclusions she had drawn, Gwen shut her eyes. "Oh, good grief! Why didn't you tell me?"

"I wanted to surprise you. And to be honest, I felt you'd think I was being silly." She began neatly to put away Gwen's lingerie. "My, what a pretty chemise. New York has such wonderful shops. Then there's the money."

"Money," Gwen repeated. Opening her eyes, she tried valiantly to follow her mother's winding train of thought. "What money?"

"Luke thinks I should sell the manuscript when I'm finished. It's—well, it's a bit crass, don't you think?"

"Oh, Mama." Gwen could only close her eyes again.

"I am sorry about not telling you and about locking my door so you wouldn't catch me writing. And about shooing you out of the house so that I could finish up. You aren't angry with me, are you?"

"No, no, I'm not angry." Gwen stared up at Anabelle's glowing face and then buried her own in her hands and laughed. "Oh, help! What a fool I've made of myself!" She rose quickly and embraced her mother. "I'm proud of you, Mama. Very proud."

"You haven't read it yet," Anabelle reminded her.

"I don't have to read it to be proud of you. And I don't think you're silly, I think you're marvelous." Drawing away slightly, she studied Anabelle's face. "Luke's right," she said, kissing both of her mother's cheeks. "You are a beautiful woman."

"Did he say that?" Anabelle dimpled. "How sweet." After patting Gwen's shoulder, she moved to the door. "I think we've solved everything nicely. Come down after you're unpacked, and I'll let you read my first chapters."

"Mama." Gwen shook her head. "I can't stay...."

"Oh, Luke." Anabelle beamed as she opened the door. "How lucky. You'll never believe the mess Gwen and I have just straightened out."

"Oh?" Luke looked past Anabelle to Gwen, then studied the open cases on her bed. "Going somewhere?"

"Yes."

"No," Anabelle said simultaneously. "Not anymore. She was going back to New York, but we solved everything nicely."

"Mama," Gwen said warningly and stepped forward.

"I've confessed all," she told Luke with a bright smile. "Gwen knows all about my secret hobby. The poor darling thought you and I were having a romance."

"Weren't we?" Luke lifted her hand to his lips.

"Oh, you devil." Anabelle patted his cheek, highly pleased. "I must get along now, but I'm sure Luke will want to hear what you told me about being in love with him."

"Mama!" The sharp retort emerged as a tragic whisper.

"I'd close the door," Anabelle suggested to Luke. "Gwen favors her privacy."

"I'll do that," Luke agreed and kissed her hand again. With a delighted blush and flutter, she disappeared.

"A truly marvelous woman," Luke commented, quietly closing the door and turning the key. He turned it over in his palm a moment, studying it, then slipped it into his pocket. Gwen decided it was better strategy not to comment. "Now, suppose you tell me what you told Anabelle about being in love with me."

Looking into his calm eyes, Gwen knew it wasn't going to be easy. Temper would not work as long as he had the key. It was vital that she remain as calm as he. "I owe you an apology," she said as she casually moved to her closet. Taking the dress Anabelle had just replaced, Gwen folded it and laid it back in the suitcase.

Luke continued to stand by the door, watching her movements. "For what, precisely?"

Gwen bit the underside of her lip hard and moved back to the closet. "For the things I said about you and Mama."

"You're apologizing for believing we were having an affair?" Luke smiled at her for the first time, and although she heard it in his voice, she did not turn to see it. "I took it as a compliment."

Turning slowly, Gwen decided to brazen it out. It was impossible, she decided, to be any more humiliated than she already was. "I'm well aware that I've made a fool of myself. And I know that I deserve to feel every bit as ridiculous as I feel. As I look back, I believe that you decided on the very first day to teach me a lesson. You never admitted you were having an affair with my mother, you simply told me it was none of my business. I felt differently at the time." Gwen paused to catch her breath, and Luke moved into the room to lean comfortably on one of the bedposts. "I was wrong and you were right. It wasn't any of my business, and you succeeded in teaching me a lesson just by letting me draw my own conclusions. These were helped along by Mama's unusual behavior and her affection for you. You could, of course, have saved me a great deal of anxiety and humiliation by explaining things, but you chose to make your point. Point taken, Mr. Powers,'' she continued as she worked herself up into a temper. ''I've been put in my place by an expert. Now, I'd like you to get out of here and leave me alone. If there's one thing I want above all else, it's never to see you again. I can only be thankful we live on opposite ends of the continent.''

Luke waited a moment while she tore two skirts out of her closet and heaved them into the case. ''Can I get a copy of that speech for my files?''

Gwen whirled, eyes flaming. ''You unfeeling, pompous boor! I've done all the groveling I'm going to do. What more do you want?''

''Was that groveling?'' he asked, lifting a brow in interest. ''Fascinating. What I want,'' he continued, ''is for you to elaborate on the statement Anabelle made before she left the room. I found it very interesting.''

''You want it all, don't you?'' Gwen snapped, slamming the lid on her first case. ''All right then, I'll give it to you. It makes little difference at this point.'' She took a breath to help the words come quickly. ''I love you. What will you do now that you know?'' she demanded, keeping her head high. ''Write it into one of your books for comic relief?''

Luke considered a moment and then shrugged. ''No. I rather think I'll marry you.''

In stunned silence, Gwen stared at him. ''I don't think that's very funny.''

''No, I doubt marriage is a funny business. I'm sure it has its moments, though. We'll have to find out.'' Straightening, he walked over and put his hands on her shoulders. ''Soon.''

''Don't touch me,'' she whispered and tried to jerk out of his hold.

''Oh yes, I'll touch you.'' He turned Gwen to face him. ''I'll do much more than touch you. Idiot,'' he said roughly when he saw her tear-drenched eyes. ''Are you so blind you can't see what you've put me through? I wanted you from the first moment I saw you. You stood there smiling at me, and I felt as though someone had hit me with a blunt instrument. I wanted to teach you a lesson, all right, but I didn't expect to learn one. I didn't expect some skinny kid to tangle herself up in my mind so that I couldn't get her out.'' He pulled her close as she stared up at him, dry eyed and fascinated. "I love you to the edge of madness," he murmured before his mouth crushed hers.

It's a dream, Gwen thought dazedly as his mouth roamed her face, teasing her skin. It must be a dream. She threw her arms around his neck and clung, praying never to wake up. "Luke," she managed before her mouth was silenced again. "Tell me you mean it," she begged as he tasted her neck. "Please tell me you mean it."

"Look at me," he ordered, taking her chin in his hand. She did and found her answer. Joy bubbled inside her and escaped in laughter. Laughing with her, Luke rested his brow against hers. "I believe I've surprised you."

"Oh, Luke." She buried her face in his shoulder, holding him as if she would never let him go. "I'm not surprised, I'm delirious." She sighed, weak from laughter, dizzy with love. "How did this happen?"

"I haven't the faintest idea." He brushed his lips over the top of her head. "Falling in love with you was not in my plans."

"Why not?" she demanded, rubbing her cheek against his. "I'm a very nice person."

"You're a child," he corrected, lost in the scent of her hair. "Do you realize what we were doing when I was your age?" He gave a quick, mystified laugh. "I was working on my second novel, and you were drawing pictures with your Crayolas."

"It's twelve years, not twenty," Gwen countered, slipping her hands under his shirt to feel the warmth of his back. "And you can hardly make an issue out of an age difference, particularly a twelve-year age difference, after all this. You don't have any double standards, do you?" she asked, lifting a brow.

Luke gave her hair a brief tug. "It's not just the years. You're so innocent, so unspoiled. Wanting you was driving me mad; then loving you only made it worse." He kissed her lightly behind the ear, and she shivered with pleasure. "Even up to last night I was determined not to take advantage of that innocence. Part of me still wants to leave you that way."

"I hope the rest of you has more sense," Gwen tossed back her head to look up at him.

"I'm serious."

"So am I." She ran a fingertip along his jawline. "Buy Bradley's portrait if you want an image."

"I already have." He smiled, caught her fingers in his and kissed them. "You don't think I'd let anyone else have it, do you?"

"Have me, too." Amusement vanished from his face as she pressed against him. "I'm a woman, Luke, not a child or an image. I love you, and I want you." Rising on her toes, she met his mouth. His hands sought her, possessed her while she trembled with excitement. Her love seemed to expand, surrounding her until there was nothing else. She pressed closer, offering everything. It was he who drew away.

"Gwen." Luke let out a long breath and shook his head. "It's difficult to remember that you're Anabelle's daughter and that she trusts me."

"I'm trying to make it impossible," she countered. She could feel the speed of his heartbeat against hers and revelled in a new sense of power. "Aren't you going to corrupt me?"

"Undoubtedly," he agreed. Framing her face with his hands, he kissed her nose. "After we're married."

"Oh." Gwen pouted a moment, then shrugged. "That's sensible, I suppose. Michael was always sensible too."

Luke's eyes narrowed at the mischief in hers. "That," he said distinctly, "was a low blow. Do you know how very near I came to pulling the phone out of the wall last night when I heard you talking to him?''

"Did you?" Gwen's face illuminated at the thought. "Were you jealous?"

"That's one way of putting it," Luke agreed.

"Well," Gwen considered carefully, trying not to smile, "I suppose I can understand that. As I said, he's a very sensible man. It's all right, though, I'm sure you're every bit as sensible as Michael."

Luke studied her carefully, but Gwen managed to keep the smile a mere hint on her lips. "Are you challenging me to kiss you into insensibility?"

"Oh, yes," she agreed and closed her eyes. "Please do."

"I never could resist a dare," Luke murmured, drawing her into his arms.

* * * * *

COMING NEXT MONTH FROM

NORA ROBERTS

#21 PARTNERS

As rival journalists competing for the latest scoop, rugged Matthew Bates and lovely Laurellie Armand found working on the same murder case as a *team* next to impossible! But as the deadline—and danger—drew inexorably closer, so did desire....

#22 SULLIVAN'S WOMAN

When darkly handsome Colin Sullivan asked penniless and ravishing Cassidy St. John to model for him, he knew he could create an enduring beauty. But Cassidy wanted to know if she could make his loving last as long.

AVAILABLE NOW:
#19 FOR NOW, FOREVER
#20 HER MOTHER'S KEEPER

In the spirit of Christmas, Silhouette invites
you to share the joy of the holiday season.

Silhouette CHRISTMAS Stories 1992

Experience the beauty of Yuletide romance with Silhouette
Christmas Stories 1992—a collection of heartwarming stories by
favorite Silhouette authors.

JONI'S MAGIC by Mary Lynn Baxter
HEARTS OF HOPE by Sondra Stanford
THE NIGHT SANTA CLAUS RETURNED by Marie Ferrarella
BASKET OF LOVE by Jeanne Stephens

This Christmas you can also receive a FREE keepsake Christmas
ornament. Look for details in all November and December
Silhouette books.

Also available this year are three popular early editions of
Silhouette Christmas Stories—1986, 1987 and 1988. Look for these
and you'll be well on your way to a complete collection of the
best in holiday romance.

Share in the celebration—with Silhouette's
Christmas gift of love.

SX92R

Silhouette

SPECIAL EDITION ™®

THE DONOVAN LEGACY
from Nora Roberts

Meet the Donovans—Morgana, Sebastian and Anastasia. Each one is unique. Each one is...special.

In September you will be *Captivated* by Morgana Donovan. In Special Edition #768, horror-film writer Nash Kirkland doesn't know what to do when he meets an actual witch!

Be *Entranced* in October by Sebastian Donovan in Special Edition #774. Private investigator Mary Ellen Sutherland doesn't believe in psychic phenomena. But she discovers Sebastian has strange powers...over her.

In November's Special Edition #780, you'll be *Charmed* by Anastasia Donovan, along with Boone Sawyer and his little girl. Anastasia was a healer, but for her it was Boone's touch that cast a spell.

Enjoy the magic of Nora Roberts. Don't miss *Captivated, Entranced* or *Charmed*. Only from Silhouette Special Edition....

───────────────────────────────────────

If you missed *Captivated* (SE#768) or *Entranced* (SE#774), order your copy now by sending your name, address, zip or postal code, along with a check or money order (please do not send cash) for $3.39 for each book ordered, plus 75¢ postage and handling ($1.00 in Canada), payable to Silhouette Books, to:

In the U.S.
3010 Walden Avenue
P.O. Box 1396
Buffalo, NY 14269-1396

In Canada
P.O. Box 609
Fort Erie, Ontario
L2A 5X3

Please specify book title(s) with your order.
Canadian residents add applicable federal and provincial taxes.

SENR-3